The ZEE FILES™

A Very Malibu Vacay

The ZEE FILES™

A Very Malibu Vacay

BY TINA WELLS

with Stephanie Smith
Illustrated by Sharifa Patrick

WEST
MARGIN
PRESS

For Eric, Arthur, Jeanette, and Wendy. —S.S.

Icon credits: surprised by xander from the Noun Project; grimacing by Martin from the Noun Project; Cosmic_Design / shutterstock.com

Library of Congress Cataloging-in-Publication Data

Names: Wells, Tina, 1980- author. | Patrick, Sharifa, illustrator.
Title: A very Malibu vacay / Tina Wells ; illustrated by Sharifa Patrick.
Description: Berkeley : West Margin Press, [2022] | Series: The Zee files ; book 4 |
    Audience: Ages 9-12. | Audience: Grades 4-6. | Summary: The Carmichaels are back
    in California for winter break and Zee cannot wait to see the old Brookdale crew, but
    despite the familiar sights and friendly faces, everything feels a little different.
Identifiers: LCCN 2022000583 (print) | LCCN 2022000584 (ebook) |
    ISBN 9781513209463 (hardback) | ISBN 9781513135038 (ebook)
Subjects: CYAC: Friendship--Fiction. | Vacation--Fiction. | California--Fiction. |
    LCGFT: Fiction.
Classification: LCC PZ7.W46846 Ve 2022 (print) | LCC PZ7.W46846 (ebook) |
    DDC [Fic]--dc23
LC record available at https://lccn.loc.gov/2022000583
LC ebook record available at https://lccn.loc.gov/2022000584

Printed in China
25 24 23 22 1 2 3 4 5

Published by West Margin Press®

WEST
MARGIN
PRESS
WestMarginPress.com

WEST MARGIN PRESS
Publishing Director: Jennifer Newens
Marketing Manager: Alice Wertheimer
Project Specialist: Micaela Clark
Editor: Olivia Ngai
Design & Production: Rachel Lopez Metzger

FSC
www.fsc.org
MIX
Paper from
responsible sources
FSC® C102842

1
READY TO GO

This is our last breakfast in London!" Mackenzie "Zee" Blue Carmichael squealed as she skipped into the kitchen. The night before, Zee had arrived back home in Notting Hill from The Hollows Creative Arts Academy, the private boarding school in the Cotswolds where she had just finished her first semester.

"Last breakfast, Zee?" Mr. Carmichael asked her.

"Well, not the last one *ever*, Dad," Zee said. "But for, like, a very long time!"

"Three weeks, Zee. We'll be gone for about three weeks. I hope you didn't pack up your entire room. We just moved in a few months ago."

The Carmichaels—Zee and her mom, dad, and twin siblings Phoebe and Connor—had finally settled into their new home after moving to London from California in the fall for Mr. Carmichael's new job. But for the winter holiday break they were heading back to California, where Zee would see her friends from her old school, Brookdale Academy, and be able to visit her favorite places to eat, play, and be merry.

Zee couldn't wait to get to Malibu, where Mrs. Carmichael rented a house for their vacation. Zee had already made plans for a sleepover or two with her best friend Chloe Lawrence-Johnson, who still went to Brookdale. Even better, Zee's other Brookdale BFF Ally Stern, who now lived in Paris, was also returning to California. Ally's family had moved to Paris a few years ago when her dad took a job at the *Financial Times*. But recently her parents separated, and this year Ally was spending the holidays with her mom in California. With all three friends finally back together, Zee had big plans for a fun-filled reunion in Malibu.

"What time is our flight?" Zee asked, sitting down at the kitchen table and excitedly digging into her eggs and toast.

"Not until later this afternoon," Mr. Carmichael said as his phone rang. "But if we're ready to go by noon, we should make good time."

Mr. Carmichael stood up to take the call in the other room, leaving Zee to eat breakfast and daydream about her winter break plans. She turned to her mother at the counter. "While we're home, let's do all of the holiday things! We can do a bunch of shopping and see all of the holiday decorations, and we can get cookies and those crazy-good hot chocolates from the mall, and watch all of the Christmas movies and parades! And then we can take the twins to go see Santa!" Zee declared. "I'm so excited to get back home. Oh, and Chloe! She has to come visit. Like, soon. Like, *immediately*! And then Ally is supposed to come and see me! This is going to be the best. Holiday. EVER!"

"Yes indeed," Mrs. Carmichael said. "And I have big plans too!

I'm going to be vlogging the entire vacation, from day to night. I have to keep creating content, you know." Mrs. Carmichael had recently become a social media influencer, thanks to her Instagram @twobycarmichael. She'd earned more than 15,000 followers from posting photos of her life as a mom of young twins, and the number of likes on her content have been even greater since documenting the family's move to London. Apparently, people liked seeing pictures of fashionable moms with their kids at places like Buckingham Palace and Harrod's.

"And of course, we have to bake cookies, and take photos of the twins in matching holiday outfits, and decorate the house," Mrs. Carmichael added. "I may need more than one tree. And... ooh, a party. We should have a party. We need. To have. A party!"

Zee rolled her eyes toward the ceiling. *Can't we just hang at the beach and have some chill time that won't be all over Instagram?* she thought. Though she liked that her mother was in a festive mood and that she was savvy at social media, Zee was annoyed at how her mother has become so obsessed with how things looked in pictures. Back in Brookdale, Mrs. Carmichael was more into gardening and crafts. Now she barely got her hands dirty.

Zee looked at her mother. "Yeah, could be fun. But Mom, do you think you'll be able to handle all that?"

"Of course! Between having Camilla and you to help, we'll be fine! And don't forget, your brother Adam is going to meet us in Malibu a few days after we arrive." Camilla was the twins' nanny and had been taking care of them while Zee was at The Hollows.

"Cool, a full house once again," Zee said. *But what about*

these parties she's talking about? Am I ever going to have a moment alone with my own mother? Or my friends?

Zee took her phone out and texted Ally, excited to touch base with her friend before she hopped on her flight.

Zee

> Ally!!! Ally in Cali! Could there be anything better?!

A few moments went by before Ally responded.

Ally

> Hi! My aunt's picking me up at the airport tonight. I'll be at her place for most of the time.

Zee

> So when can you come to the house?

Ally

> I hope soon!

Zee

> OK, well, we will be there the entire time and I will have your bed ready, hahahaha!!

Ally

> Yes! Best holiday ever! Or at least better than last year!

Zee

> Yes! Where's your mom, BTW?

Zee got up from the kitchen table and went to her room to pack the last of her things. She had spent very little time in her own bedroom in her London house after enrolling at The Hollows, since she lived at the boarding school full-time. But Notting Hill was starting to feel more like home. And her room now had something to make it even more comforting, a valued piece that had recently arrived in the mail after many months—her treasured acoustic guitar. The movers had forgotten to put it in the truck when the Carmichaels left California, so they had mailed it off to London months ago. But thanks to cargo shipping, it had taken forever to get to Notting Hill.

Zee smiled when she spotted the guitar waiting for her in the corner of the room, sitting upright on its stand. "There you are!" she exclaimed. "Come to mama!"

She played a few chords on the instrument, humming along to the song she'd recently written for The Hollows Creative Arts Festival where Zee had performed a solo. She couldn't wait to bring the guitar back to campus and jam on it in her dorm room. Her roommate, Jameela Chopra, was usually at ballet practice after school anyway, so Zee thought she could squeeze in some guitar playing while Jameela was out.

Zee thought about how she wanted to create new songs with her pal Jasper Chapman, who produced music and was her best guy friend at The Hollows. And she thought about the guy who had helped her put together the melody for the song she had performed, and with whom she had a brief but complex relationship with: Archie Saint John, a handsome and talented guitarist and fellow year nine student. He had taken a quick liking to Zee, and the two became fast friends and eventually boyfriend and girlfriend, which meant they had hung out together. A lot. Archie had liked hanging around Zee so much, too much, that she quickly felt smothered and broke things off with him. They were just friends now. *And that's a good place for us to be,* Zee thought to herself.

For now, it was time to head to California, back to her old stomping grounds and far from Archie Saint John. She put the guitar back down on its stand and finished packing up the last of her things.

• • •

> **Hey girl! Weather still nice in Cali?
> I'm bringing all the summer clothes!**

Tossing her phone on her bed, Zee shoved a few more T-shirts into her suitcase. She packed a pair of sandals and another pair of flip flops, and paused. Then she added yet another pair of sandals and zipped up the oversized suitcase. "That should do it," she said to herself.

Zee dragged her suitcase down to the front door. Mrs. Carmichael was running around the house getting together the last of her things while Camilla got the twins dressed for the plane ride. "The twins have the most luggage of all of us, it seems," said Zee, eyeing their two car seats, two strollers, and two carry-on bags full of clothes, snacks, and toys stacked by the door.

"I'll load up the car," Mr. Carmichael said, and began stuffing the family's luggage into a black SUV. Mr. Carmichael made several trips while Mrs. Carmichael seemed to add a small bag, snack, or jacket to the pile of goods each time he returned to the house to grab another handful.

Finally, after thirty minutes of packing up the car, the family was ready to go a few minutes before noon. Mr. Carmichael began to pull the car away from the house while in the backseat Zee fished in her backpack for her headphones, phone, and lip gloss. "WAAIIITTT!" she cried out.

"What, dear?" Mrs. Carmichael asked.

"I forgot something!" Zee cried. "Really important!"

"We can't bring your guitar, Zee," Mr. Carmichael said. "We're already over our baggage weight limit as it is."

"No, more important! I need to go back inside."

Zee hopped out of the backseat, and her mother followed to unlock the door and let her daughter back inside the house. "Zee, hurry up, we don't want to be late!" Mrs. Carmichael said.

Zee ran up the stairs to her bedroom on the third floor. She checked her nightstand next to her bed. *Not there.* Then she looked in her backpack, rifling through the books, notebooks, and pens she had brought home from school. *Not there either.* She plopped down on her bean bag. *I need to find it before I go,* she thought.

She looked around her room, her eyes panning from the bed to the closet, then to the window on the opposite side of the room and her desk. She looked at the shelf above her desk. *Nope, not there, or there, or there.*

She let out a frustrated exhale. *What could I have done with it?* she thought. Zee walked toward her desk...

"There it is!" she exclaimed. "How did it get down there?"

"It" was a brand-new journal, like the one that Zee used to keep all her thoughts, worries, fears, and emotional observances. Since transferring to The Hollows, Zee has been struggling with anxiety and has been regularly seeing the school therapist, Dr. Emma Banks. Dr. Banks had recommended journaling for Zee to help keep track of her feelings. Zee's journal was now a safe haven for her thoughts, the ones that she was too nervous to express out loud or simply didn't want anyone else to know. Zee thought something similar would be the perfect gift for Ally, who wrote for her school literary journal and always seemed to have deep thoughts.

Zee stuffed the colorful book under her arm and turned quickly back out of the room. She bounded down the stairs, where her mother was waiting by the banister. "Did you get what you needed?" Mrs. Carmichael asked.

"Yes," Zee said, relieved. "Oh wait, where's my passport?"

"I have that," Mrs. Carmichael said. "And Phoebe's and Connor's. And your father's. Now let's go before we miss our flight."

Zee and her mother hurried back to the car, quickly jumped into their seats, and rode to the airport. Zee smiled as she watched the sights and sounds of Notting Hill whiz by. As new and interesting as London was, she was excited to switch out her view of old buildings and snow with palm trees and sunshine for the next three weeks in Malibu.

2

L.A. BOUND

*A*fter three hours at Heathrow Airport, which included stopping in various shops to buy candy, magazines, and extra bottles of water, the Carmichaels loaded onto their flight. Zee settled into her seat next to her mother and grabbed her headphones. She was ready to throw a blanket over herself and watch a few cheesy plane movies, read some magazines, and catch a nap somewhere in between during the eleven-hour flight.

Before the plane took off, Zee got a text from Chloe.

Chloe

> Weather is grand! Text when you land. Can't wait to see you. Neither can Landon and Kathi, haha!

Zee raised her eyebrows. Chloe had mentioned two of the people at Brookdale Academy that she felt most hesitant about seeing. Landon Beck was her friend who became something more and then became something weird. Was it a crush? Was it more? Zee still couldn't describe it. Whatever it was, Zee and Landon felt the same way for exactly three minutes, but Zee's feelings faded quickly while Landon's feelings lingered. Zee ended up leaving Brookdale without really saying goodbye and had been wondering if that was the right thing to do ever since.

Kathi Barney was another story. Kathi and Zee were frenemies at Brookdale. Kathi was the sort of girl who smiled at your face when she wanted something, then talked about you behind your back. She was always looking for attention—from teachers to friends (Zee's friends, in particular)—and desperately wanted to sing the lead in Zee's Brookdale band, The Beans. But Zee was the stronger performer, so Kathi was relegated to singing backup. Zee had not planned on seeing Kathi much during her time in Malibu, which would be a relief. *But if Landon wanted to pay me a visit, I wouldn't mind,* Zee thought to herself.

• • •

The plane leveled off at 30,000 feet, and the flight attendants began serving snacks and passing out headphones to passengers. Mrs. Carmichael was busy tending to the twins as they squirmed in their seats. Camilla read a book to Connor while Mrs. Carmichael fed Phoebe.

"Zee," Mr. Carmichael called. "They have *Home Alone* on the media system." It was one of Zee's favorite holiday films. Zee smiled and started to flip through the menu items on the screen in front of her.

About an hour into the movie, Zee drifted off into another world, a place she had been before. It was Brookdale, her old neighborhood, with its tree-lined streets and tidy houses, and kids riding their bikes and rollerblading toward her old school, Brookdale Academy. Zee was sitting in her mom's old Prius, headed to the school. She was excited to be on campus again.

Mrs. Carmichael pulled up in front of the school. But something was off. There were no students outside. No teachers. It looked like there was no school today.

"You're sure it's not a holiday?" Zee asked.

"I'm sure, Zee! It's Brookdale. Go on, go see your friends!" Mrs. Carmichael said.

Zee raised an eyebrow at her mother, then slowly opened the car door and got out.

Hesitantly, Zee walked toward the school building but heard no one. "Have a good day at school," Mrs. Carmichael called behind her. Zee looked over her shoulder and saw her mother was already driving off.

Where is everyone? Zee thought to herself.

Zee looked at her watch. *Oh. My. Lanta!* It was already 10 a.m. *Why hadn't Mom told me I was two hours late for school? She made it sound like everything was going to be awesome.* Zee raced to the front door and yanked hard on the door handle. It was locked. "Hello?!" Zee called, trying to get someone's attention.

She could see a few students in the hallway just past the entrance, walking too fast to notice a flustered Zee at the door. Zee rattled the door handle, trying to signal to someone to let her inside, but no one came. Zee cupped her two hands around her face and pushed her head against the glass, peering down the empty school hallway. She was an alumna, for crying out loud, a proud former student! Her picture was on the wall of the library along with the other Beans band members. Why wouldn't anyone let her in?

Finally, a student walking by saw Zee knocking on the door. He didn't recognize her, but he walked closer to get a better look. It was Landon, Zee's former crush. He looked confused, then started laughing and pointing at her. Then he called a friend over, and the friend laughed and pointed too. Another boy came over, then a girl Zee didn't recognize, then another. Soon, there were ten kids laughing and pointing at her.

"Why won't you let me in?" Zee asked. "I just want to come back inside!"

Then Kathi Barney joined in with the crowd, laughing and pointing at Zee. Soon, dozens of kids were treating Zee as if she were a clown trapped inside a cage too small for her. Zee didn't understand what was going on, but she yanked and yanked on the door handle, and the louder and longer she banged and pulled on the door, the louder and longer the laughter from the students inside grew. Finally, Zee screamed:

"Let me in!"

Suddenly, Zee felt a hand grip her arm. "Zee? Zee," the voice said. Zee tried to shake herself free of the grip. She pushed herself away, jolting up in her seat. Taking a breath, Zee saw her startled mother staring at her. "You okay?" Mrs. Carmichael asked.

Zee looked around, confused. She was not in Brookdale. She was on the flight to Los Angeles, still on the plane, still in her seat. "Yeah. Fine. Just a dream," Zee said. A very bad dream. A nightmare of epic proportions. *Kathi Barney and Landon laughing at me? Oh man, I hope my reunion at Brookdale doesn't go that bad,* she thought.

Zee leaned forward and pulled out her journal and pen from inside her backpack. She clicked the pen and started to write furiously, not wanting to forget the dream before she could record it in her journal.

Why did I have a nightmare about Brookdale Academy? It was my happy place. Where my friends and old bandmates were! Why did I dream all of a sudden about being an outsider? Am I an outsider now? Are people going to be mean to me when I arrive? Ugh, mylanta!

Zee tucked the journal back into her backpack. Then she pulled the blanket back over her body and up to her shoulders, eventually falling back asleep.

• • •

After their long flight to Los Angeles, the Carmichaels took a large SUV to their rental home in Malibu, an hour's drive away from the airport. They piled out of the car in front of a large rectangular house that was mostly windows, right on the beach. Zee walked into the house and her mouth dropped wide open.

"Whoooaaaa! I cannot believe this is ours for the entire winter break!" she exclaimed.

Zee turned her head from side to side to take in the full view of the two-story open-concept home. From the front entry, she could see the oversized kitchen, family room, and dining area, and beyond that the patio, pool, and gazebo outside overlooking the ocean. A grand piano was tucked into the den opposite the family room. The property manager walked her parents through the house and its grounds while Zee strolled slowly across the light wood floors.

Phoebe and Connor ran ahead of her, eager to get their shoes off so they could jump on the oversized couches. Zee walked into the family room after them. "I cannot wait to have Chloe and Ally here!" she said.

Zee took out her phone and started filming short video clips of the house, narrating the scene as if she were on an HGTV series. She then added the clips to the Zee Files, the secret digital scrapbook where Zee, Ally, and Chloe uploaded their texts, photos, videos, and other messages for each other so they could keep in touch. *This place is amazing!* Zee wrote in a caption.

She walked past the kitchen, with its shiny, new silver appliances and white cabinets and countertops, to the dining area, where a long, rectangular table was already set for a group of ten. "This place was made for entertaining," Mrs. Carmichael said as she peered in. "We should ask the neighbors to join us for dinner just because we have space at the table."

Between the dining room and kitchen, Zee spotted a clear space. "Mom, that's the perfect place for the tree," Zee yelled out.

"For one of them anyway, yes!" her mother yelled back. The twins were already running down the hallways, looking for small treats and toys to play with as Camilla chased after them.

The family meandered through the large shared spaces and the bedrooms before making their way outside, where the air smelled salty and fresh. A large grill was built into the outdoor kitchen and bar area. Zee immediately ran to one of the loungers by the pool. She sat down and lay back, letting the sun beam down on her face. "Ahhhhh," she said.

Zee wasn't the only one who was recording the house's features on her phone—Mrs. Carmichael captured every moment for her Instagram feed. She even took footage of the property manager explaining some of the house's key features. Mrs. Carmichael flashed the camera over to Zee.

"Mom, can ya stop? Can we just move in already?" Zee said. "Where's my bedroom?"

"Which bedroom do you want, the one across from the pool?"

"Absolutely!" Zee hustled to her room, rolling her suitcase

behind her, and stopped at the first door off the family room that was across the pool. The large door was heavy, but it swung open to a light and airy bedroom. Zee gasped at the sight of the oversized bed, the white fluffy comforter that looked like cotton candy, and the flat screen television on top of the dresser. Zee walked over to the bed and turned her back, then fell onto the comforter, sinking into the mattress. "This is heavenly," she sighed.

Just when she felt her body relax into the bed, Zee got a text from Chloe and smiled.

Chloe

I'm coming tomorrow. Get ready for me!

3

BFF REUNION

Zee started to unpack her things in her room for the next three weeks, carefully shaking out her T-shirts and shorts and placing them in the large drawer underneath the television. *Netflix. All. Night. Long*, she thought to herself. She placed her shoes in a tidy row in the closet. Then she texted Chloe and Ally.

Zee

> Guys, this place is ridiculous! We can have you and your entire families stay over all at once!

As Zee started humming the melody for one of her favorite Christmas songs, she saw her journal sticking out of her backpack. She looked around and took in her surroundings: California, the festive season, family together. The holiday spirit started to bubble up in her chest. *Maybe I'll write my own Christmas song*, she thought.

Zee grabbed the journal and sat on her bed. She thought back to her favorite holidays growing up as a kid. The year her parents got her that first guitar. The small toy one that had only four strings. That was the year her brother Adam got his first video game system and she had watched him play it for hours during winter break. "Watch and learn, little lady," Adam had said any time Zee asked if she could play.

Zee started writing down all the things about the holidays she loved. Christmas trees. Gingerbread men. Mint candies.

Snow is falling, fire's burning bright.
Mom's baking, Christmas movie night.
Candy canes, fairy lights, candles and cheer
Home sweet home
Holidays are here.

Zee smiled as she hummed along to the song while looking around for her Christmas pajamas. She had brought several pairs with her—her mom had bought everyone a pair for a family photo, plus Zee wanted to do a photo shoot with Ally and Chloe, so they had coordinated to buy the same candy cane–striped pajamas for their sleepover. Zee slipped on that pair now, the material light and breathable, just right for holiday nights near the beach. Then she grabbed her phone and texted Ally.

Zee

Girl! This house is amazing. When can we hang?

Not sure. Mom's being super weird. Need to ask my aunt who makes plans for us every two seconds.

I didn't fly all this way to hang out with just them. This was supposed to be OUR reunion.

Exactly! Keep me posted. Chloe's coming over now.

• • •

The doorbell was loud enough to get the attention of everyone in the house, but it was nothing in comparison to the high-pitched shrieks that came out of Chloe and Zee's mouths when they saw each other for the first time since Zee moved to London.

"It's *soooooooooooo* good to see you!" Chloe said. The friends hugged each other tightly.

"It's *amaaaaaaaaaaazing* to see you!" Zee said, taking a step back to take a good look at her friend. Chloe was wearing bike shorts and an oversized jersey, and her hair was pulled back into two long French braids on the sides of her head. "OMG, you look amazing! What, are you wearing makeup?"

"No!" Chloe said. "Not like *real* makeup."

"Are those your real lashes?" Zee asked.

"Of course these are my real lashes! All I have on is lip gloss."

To Zee, Chloe looked like she'd grown into a teenager overnight. Chloe looked more glowy and mature than Zee remembered, just like Ally did when Zee saw her in Paris for the first time after a while. *Is she wearing a bra? That bump on her shoulder under her shirt, is that a bra strap?* Zee wondered. *Geez, is everyone going to leave me here in the awkward phase?*

Zee felt a pang of insecurity growing in her chest, like her best friend had gotten a makeover and forgotten to invite her. "You look like you just left a photo shoot for *Teen Vogue!*" Zee said.

"Really? I haven't done anything new. Okay, maybe the braids, but nothing *new* new!"

Zee shook herself out of her thoughts. "Come in! I can't wait to tell you everything," she said to her friend. "Let me show you around!"

The girls walked toward the family room, where the television was currently turned to *Peppa Pig* for the twins.

"Wow, this house is amazing!" Chloe said. "Like this would be a dope location for a music video. Was this one of those TikTok mansions last summer? That gazebo thing looks familiar."

"I don't think so," Zee said. "My mom would have mentioned it. Come, I'll show you my room. Then we can go by the pool and chill."

The girls walked down the long hallway to the left of the kitchen to Zee's big room. "This is fantastic! I may not go home," Chloe said as she looked around.

"Don't! Stay here all Christmas!"

"Mom wouldn't dare leave me for a whole two weeks."

Zee sat on the bed. "So what's going on? Have I missed anything?"

Chloe unzipped her bag and took out her swimsuit, a cover-up, and flip flops. "Haven't I told you everything already? We text just about every day and put all of our photos in the Zee Files!"

"Yeah, but maybe new stuff has happened! Maybe you forgot stuff!"

"Mm, I sent you the photos of me dressed like a slasher cheerleader for Halloween, right?" Chloe said, thinking. "And Marcus dressed as a slasher lawyer—typical—and of course he looked good even though he was dressed like a monster."

"You still have a crush on him?"

"Crush? No! Me?" Chloe became flustered. "No. Well, I think he's cool. But I'm not like you were with Mr. Archie in London. How is he, by the way?"

"I have no idea," Zee said, raising an eyebrow in disbelief at how quickly Chloe deflected the subject away from herself to Zee. "I haven't heard from him since I left."

"Oh. Well, bye, boy. On to the next," Chloe said.

"Yeah. Exactly."

"Have you heard from Jasper?" Chloe asked.

"We texted a little bit," Zee said. "He's in London with his family. All good."

"Right," Chloe said. "What about Ally? When is she coming? When are we having our girls' reunion?"

"She's in L.A. with her mom and aunt celebrating Hanukkah," Zee said. "I haven't heard much from her either."

"You know what would be awesome?" Chloe said. "Maybe we could get a jam session with the old Beans crew together. Like, when you come over to my place, maybe Ally can come and—oh wait, we don't have Jasper... hmm."

"Oh, right," Zee said. "Half the band has moved."

"We broke up because you moved!"

"That's not true!"

"I know, just kidding," Chloe said. "Ooh, I know what we could do! Why don't you come to class with me sometime next week and see everybody back at school? We have one more week before break. I can ask for permission for you to come as my guest. We can say you're shadowing me."

Zee's eyes grew big. She thought back to her nightmare on the plane ride from London. "Do you think anyone would remember me?"

"Of course! I told you Landon and Kathi have been asking about you. And Mr. P would love to see you. And your other teachers! And the head of school. You were such the goody two shoes at school, I'm sure everyone would love to see you."

Zee thought about it. She smiled at hearing that people missed her. *I wonder if Landon feels the same way?* she wondered.

"Yeah, that would be funsies!" Zee said. "I can come back and see all the old friends."

"And then we could do a jam session in Mr. P's class! You could have your old spot again and make Kathi Barney so annoyed. It will be awesome!" Chloe said.

"Yeah!" Zee said, her eyes getting wide. "When you go to school on Monday, ask. And I'll ask my mom. She'll probably have to take me. Ooh, let's call Ally! Maybe she'll want to come too!"

Chloe took out her phone and tried to FaceTime Ally. The ringing went on for what seemed like a minute. Finally, a grainy image of Ally's face popped up. "Hiii," she said.

"Hiii. Where are you and what are you doing?" Chloe asked.

"I'm at my aunt's and I'm bored off my face," Ally said.

"Come here!" Zee said.

"I wish, but, like, they just want to stay at home and chill. I like being home, but... my mom's not even here."

"Where is she?" Chloe asked.

"She's out."

"Out where?" Zee asked.

"Oh, it's complicated. Anyway, what are you two doing?"

"Chilling and making all of our holiday plans. You need to come and visit!" Zee said.

"Hey, Zee's coming with me to school next week," Chloe added. "Maybe you could do that too!"

"That sounds like fun. I'll ask my mom," Ally said.

"'Ask! And make your plans to come see me. Chloe's here until tomorrow, unless she moves in. Which she should."

"Okay, okay," Ally said. "I miss you guys."

"Miss you too, but not for long!" Chloe and Zee said. The

girls hung up then headed outside to sit on the loungers, taking in the California sun on the first day of their Malibu holiday reunion.

4

BACK TO BROOKDALE

*A*fter a quick dip in the pool, Chloe and Zee explored—and took photos in—every inch of the Malibu home. They jumped on the trampoline in the backyard and ate snacks on the pool loungers. Then they scoped out each bathroom to see which one had the best light and lip-synched to a bunch of Christmas carols while they made up dance routines. Afterwards, they had dinner in the living room and plotted how to put up Christmas decorations. They reminisced about their Christmases of the past ("Mom pulled out the pictures of us sitting on Santa's lap at the mall the other day!" Chloe said) and made homemade hot chocolates and sipped them while watching movies in Zee's room. In between, they took dozens of photos and posted everything to the Zee Files, leaving commentary for Ally so she would still feel like she was right there with the girls.

On Monday morning, Chloe treated Zee's potential visit to Brookdale Academy as if she were bringing the president to the school. Dressed in ironed black slacks with a white button-down shirt and a blazer, Chloe went to the head of school Dr. Harrison's office to ask for special permission for Zee to come with her to classes for a day. Chloe had signatures from her parents and from Zee's parents to authorize the visit. Bracing herself, Chloe expected a lengthy negotiation to let a former student back into Brookdale Academy, but there wasn't any argument in the end.

"Of course she can come, so long as one of her parents drops her off first," Dr. Harrison said.

Chloe immediately texted Zee the good news.

Chloe

Girl, you're in!

Zee

I know! My mom called the school this morning and asked if I could come back and visit.

Chloe

Oh. Well, I'm your chaperone for the day. So make me look good!

• • •

An excited Zee woke up ahead of her alarm the next day, ready to look her most dazzling for her visit back to Brookdale Academy. She wanted to appear as if things were going well, if not awesome, in London for her. But she also yearned to connect with her old friends and feel as if no time had gone by since her last walk down Brookdale's familiar halls. She put on a white polo shirt and a black pleated skirt with her white Veja sneakers. Not a uniform, but still polished.

Mrs. Carmichael agreed to drive Zee to the school and was eager to see if things had changed since they were last there. "And of course, I want to take some footage of my baby's return to her old school as well," Mrs. Carmichael said.

The drive from Malibu to Brookdale was about a half hour. Zee and Chloe texted each other and Ally the entire time.

Zee

Ally! Want us to pick you up on the way? We can have a full reunion! Would be epic!

Ally never responded. *She must be busy with her family,* Zee thought to herself.

As Mrs. Carmichael pulled the car into the school parking lot, something in Zee's chest fluttered. All the great memories of her time at Brookdale came flooding back to her: lunches in the cafeteria, school assemblies and singalongs, their annual field trips. Zee quietly hoped her friends and teachers remembered her as much as she remembered them.

Brookdale Academy was known for being eco-friendly and using sustainable or recycled materials on campus. As Zee walked through the building doors, some things were just as she remembered—the recessed LED lighting, the recycled steel used for the ductwork and beams. There were signs for afterschool clubs like the Girls Scouts, 4H, and Earth to Brookdale, a club that does activities to help save the earth. Looking around, Zee recognized a few of the students who were in grades below her when she was last there. But there was a vibe that was different. Zee fidgeted. Maybe seeing Chloe and Mr. P would ease that feeling.

Zee and her mother walked into the front office. "Hi! I'm Mackenzie Carmichael," Zee said to the receptionist.

"How are you, Mackenzie? I remember you from your band performances," said the woman behind the desk. She seemed nice and had curly brown hair and a big smile. "Dr. Harrison will be with you in a bit."

Zee looked around the office, gazing at the school achievement awards and announcements hanging on the wall. Not much in the main office has changed either. The phone rang constantly and computer keys clacked loudly as the front office staffers typed.

A tall woman in a suit with a familiar face appeared. "Mackenzie, long time no see! How are you? Hello, Mrs. Carmichael," Dr. Harrison greeted.

"Hi, Dr. Harrison. Same to you!" Zee said, shaking her hand. "Wow, it's so trippy being here again."

"We're glad to have you for a visit. I see that you're here to shadow Chloe Lawrence-Johnson, is that right?"

"Yep! We got special permission for me to go with her to a few of her classes today," Zee replied.

"Of course, of course. Chloe should be here any minute to meet you, and then you two can go to your first class together."

"Great," Mrs. Carmichael said, then turned to Zee. "Listen, while you're at school, I'm going into town to get some errands done. I'll pick you up here after lunch. That sound good?"

"Yup, sounds good."

Just then, Chloe burst through the front door of the office, her arms wide open. "Hey hey, my girl is back!" she said, announcing Zee's presence to the entire office in case they missed her.

"Hi!" Zee said, hugging her friend.

"I already went to music class and saved us seats in the front row. Mr. P is expecting us, so let's go!" Chloe grabbed Zee's hand and guided her toward the door. Zee turned back to give her mother a quick wave before following quickly behind Chloe.

Chloe and Zee walked through the halls shoulder to shoulder, waving hello to some friends as they passed by. "This place is starting to feel like home again," Zee said.

"Do you remember, like, everything?" Chloe asked.

"I remember a lot, that's for sure," Zee said, looking around at what seemed to be new art on the main hallway corridor. "Don't remember that though."

"Yeah, we also got some new vending machines, and there's a couple of new classes. And obviously we have a new student body president. But pretty much everything is just as you left it."

Chloe and Zee arrived at the music classroom, and Zee smiled at the nostalgic feelings that came. She remembered the seats set up in a semicircle shape, the larger instruments in the back with the smaller ones toward the front. She waved to a few recognizable faces as she walked through class, like Bobby Thomas who played the oboe ("Yo! Zee's back!" he called out), and Michael Wyatt who played violin. Missy Vasi also gave a wave ("Welcome back, Zee!" she said politely), and Conrad Mitori, who played keyboard, gave Zee a quick head nod and a smile, as did Jen Calverez. Zee followed Chloe to their seats, but then saw a familiar yet undesirable face sitting on the other side of her friend. Kathi Barney smirked as Zee came closer.

"Mackenzie Carmichael," Kathi said.

"Kathi Barney," Zee said in response.

"My oh my, it's been a minute," Kathi said, raising an eyebrow. "As I told Chloe last week, I sort of missed you. I mean, it's just, like, not the same without you buzzing about, singing and talking all the time."

"Well, I missed you too, Kathi," Zee said, enunciating every word. "You good?"

"Great," Kathi said. "I've been sitting lead on most of our school assemblies, and there was talk of me taking over The Beans in your absence."

Chloe piped in. "No, there hasn't, and not a chance, Kathi. The Beans aren't the same without Zee."

"Right," Kathi said. "Anyway, I have been working on my songwriting, and I'd hope, Zee, that you've been working on yours while you've been gone."

"Of course I have, Kathi," Zee said, rolling her eyes. "I go to a creative arts boarding school. I study music, I perform music. Music is all I do. In fact, I just performed in our school talent show. It was brilliant!"

"Brilliant, huh?"

"Yes, quite," Zee said. "And that was without having my guitar on me. I just got in the mail, so now I can jam properly with my mates."

"With your 'mates'?" Kathi looked at her. "Gosh, Zee, you really sound like a true British person. You sound very... what's the word? Posh?"

"Oh, yeah, I guess I have picked up some of the local slang," Zee said.

"Well, can't wait to see what you've been working on in

class today." Kathi smirked as Zee sat down. She looked away from Zee and turned her head toward the chalkboard.

Mr. P, Brookdale Academy's affable music teacher, entered the classroom wearing a white button-down shirt and khaki pants. He gave Zee a nod and walked over to her seat. Zee noted how casual he looked compared to her uniformed teachers back at The Hollows.

"Welcome back, Zee. Good to see you," he said.

"Mr. P!" Zee replied. "Thanks for letting me crash class!"

He smiled at her. "Can't wait to hear you perform again. I think your bandmates feel the same."

Just then, Landon Beck, wearing a white button-down with his sleeves rolled up halfway, blue trousers, and Vans sneakers, walked into class. Zee's heart skipped a beat. She looked him over. He locked eyes with her, and the two of them stumbled over their words.

"Zee, wow, I..." Landon stuttered. "I didn't know you were coming today. I mean, I knew you were coming, but not which day."

"Um, hi. Yes, um, well, it was sort of a surprise," Zee stammered. "Chloe arranged for me to hang out with her this morning at school. Guess I'm the guest at Brookdale Academy for the day!"

"Cool," Landon said, a smile growing slowly across his face. "I like it. How have you been? You look the same."

The corner of Zee's mouth dropped in disappointment. She didn't want to look the same, she wanted to look radiant, beautiful, mature! "I've been good!" Zee answered, perking up to stay as upbeat as possible. "I mean, I'm good... I... um... it's... um, yeah, we should catch up or something. Or we should... um, you know...?"

Mr. P clapped his hands. "All right, class, let's get started. We're going to practice our song for the assembly, 'Lean on Me.'"

Everyone moved their seats around into the right formation for the song, then looked at Mr. P. On his cue, Zee started to jam with her old classmates, banging to the beat on a tambourine she grabbed from the music cabinet, falling back into rhythm with them effortlessly. It was like she found her old spot in a lineup, no problem. After their first run-through, Mr. P looked at Zee. "Nice work, Zee. Great!"

"Thanks!" she said eagerly.

Mr. P then gave a short lecture on the song. Zee listened intently as he went over their performance notes, her eyes stealing a few glances at Landon in between. The class practiced the song once more before Mr. P called it a day.

"You like jamming with the old crew?" Chloe asked her friend with a smile.

"Yeah, I wish we could do this again," Zee said as she looked

around. An idea popped into her head and Zee grabbed Chloe's arm. "Oh! What if everyone came to my house in Malibu for a jam session? That house is huge, so we could definitely fit the entire class. We could do it this weekend! And maybe my mom can make some food and we can have a holiday jam session!"

"Sounds fun!" Chloe said.

There was a minute left in class when Mr. P made an announcement. "Let's give a big send-off to Zee for coming back and visiting us today. Did it feel good to be back, Zee?"

"Yes, sir!" Zee said, then stood up on her seat and addressed the class. "So good that I want to invite the gang back to my place for a reunion! We have so much space, we can jam there and roast marshmallows in between sets! And Mr. P, you should come too!"

Everyone started to chatter. "I like the sound of that!" one student said. "Malibu jamboree!" shouted another.

Zee looked at her former music teacher. "Mr. P, can you swing it?"

He smiled. "If you get your mother's permission first."

Zee froze, then put her finger to her temple. "Oh yeah, I guess I should have thought of that. But I'm sure she won't mind. Our house is HUGE. The whole school can sleep there!"

Chloe looked at Zee in disbelief. "You think your mom will be okay with this?"

"Sure, why not?" Zee said with a shrug. She hoped her mother would sign on to her party plans. Inviting a few dozen kids over—with instruments—would really make for a full house. Zee followed everyone out of the classroom, shaking off worries about her mom's reaction. *What's not to like about a holiday singalong?* Zee thought to herself.

5
AN ACCIDENTAL PARTY

After lunch with Chloe in the cafeteria, Zee waited for Mrs. Carmichael back at the school's front office. Zee jumped up at the sight of her mother coming through the door, eager to tell her the news.

"Mom! Mr. P and the rest of the music gang want to come to our house to Malibu for a jam session! Would that be okay?"

Mrs. Carmichael looked at Zee, puzzled. "This sounds like a party."

Zee looked at her mother. *Uh oh*, Zee thought. *I have to tell my mom I invited the entire eighth grade band to my house without her permission. This may not end well.* "No, it doesn't have to be, like, a huge party. It was just an excuse for all of us to get together and jam like we used to before," she said.

Mrs. Carmichael's eyebrows raised higher on her face. "This still sounds like a party."

Zee feared she was about to get in trouble. "No," she said slowly, "more like a small gathering of my old schoolmates. And a jam session. I need to practice my music during the break, and what better way to do that? I mean, I didn't mean to invite people over without your permission. It kind of just slipped out."

Mrs. Carmichael looked skeptically at her daughter. "How many people did you invite from Brookdale before you asked me about this party?"

Zee got flustered. She knew she had invited way more people than a casual hangout. "I guess I invited the whole music class."

"Right. So it's a party," Mrs. Carmichael said. Her mouth grew into a smile. "And since we're having a party, we should do a big Malibu winter wonderland type of party!"

Zee's face froze in surprise. She didn't expect her mother to be more excited about this gathering than she was. "Um, are you serious?"

"Absolutely! I was looking for a great excuse to do a holiday party," Mrs. Carmichael said. "We'll need to plan the menu, decor, theme, custom beverages—the works! Oh, we could make festive treats, or we can barbecue. Maybe we'll get catering and hire a company to do the festive holiday decorations. Better yet, we can have a decorating station! And a snow globe area... or maybe we can bring in fake snow by one of those local businesses and make the entire backyard look like the North Pole!"

Zee looked at her mom, overwhelmed. "But I really was thinking just a little jam session..."

"Let's invite anyone you want!" Mrs. Carmichael said. "In fact, invite the parents too! The kids will need to get to our house somehow and that means parents driving them out there, so we might as well welcome the parents to stay. Oh, maybe I'll invite a few of my friends. Like Ally's mom, and the Harrolds. I haven't seen them since we moved!"

Mrs. Carmichael's mind was running a mile a minute and Zee could not keep up. "That all sounds amazing, Mom. But how are you going to do all of that? You really don't need to go all the way out," Zee said.

"Nonsense!" Mrs. Carmichael said. "This isn't going way out—this is going all in! This is decking the halls! It's spreading some holiday cheer!"

Zee trailed behind her mother in shock as they walked out to the parking lot. Zee had wanted to have her old music classmates over for a singalong and maybe a few Christmas cookies and hot chocolate, just like old times in Brookdale. But a snow globe? Fake snow? A holiday extravaganza? With her mother acting like Mrs. Claus and the whole thing probably broadcasted on her social media channel?

This is way more than I wanted, thought Zee as she wondered how in all that is holy and bright a casual reunion of The Beans turned into a huge holiday bash.

• • •

When Zee and her mother returned to the Malibu house, Zee slinked off to her room and flopped herself down on the bed to let her heavy mind think. She took a big breath in, then exhaled slowly, hoping to find some peace in the silence. She sat up and grabbed her journal to write down her frustrated feelings that her mom was going to put way more stress on this event than needed.

This was supposed to be The Beans' reunion! A chill gathering with my old friends where we could jam and laugh and just catch up by the beach. But now, Mom has made it into a film set for her to get content for her Instagram feed. What if I don't want to be on her feed? What if my friends don't?

And what about the planning of this big bash? She's totally made all the decisions! Was she going to ask me what I thought of the decorations? Or what food I wanted? I mean, geez... I have ideas too!

Zee took a deep breath and fluttered her lips as she exhaled. She thought back to that holiday song she'd been working on in her journal, the one inspired by happy times and family traditions, particularly those with her mom.

Zee opened the journal to the page where she'd written the lyrics. She scribbled down some thoughts.

This season looks different from the days of old
Everything sparkles like glitter and gold
But the special magic doesn't feel the same
Sad to say, it's starting to feel kinda lame...

Wow, Zee realized, *I've never felt this sad on the holidays.* She closed the journal and flopped back on her bed.

• • •

Before dinnertime, Zee's phone vibrated. It was a text message from Landon. *He still has my number?* she wondered.

Landon

> **What's up? Good 2CU today.**

Zee smiled and decided to wait a minute before responding. *I don't want to seem too eager*, she thought. Instead of texting back right away, she went to the bathroom to fix her hair, put on lip gloss, and organize her hair accessories. Then she returned to her room and picked up her phone again.

Zee

> **Thanks! U2. You still have my number?**

Landon

> **Got it from Chloe. So, serious about that party?**

> Yep, my mom already made invitations online. Asked me for phone numbers and emails of the kids and parents. You'll get one.

Landon

> Thanks. Got any time to hang before the party? Like after school tomorrow? At Jeni's?

Zee felt a tingling in her chest. She hadn't had an extended conversation with Landon since she left for London. She was nervous about how they had ended things, but she wasn't sure she was prepared to rehash the whole thing over ice cream.

Landon

> We could chat about London and stuff.

Sounds innocent enough, Zee thought. She texted him back.

Zee

> Sure, I'll ask my mom if she can bring me that way tomorrow. I'll text you after I talk to her.

Landon

> Cool.

Landon

Zee tossed her phone down on the bed. She tried to hold back the smile creeping across her face, but it was too late. Thinking about seeing Landon for the first time alone over ice cream brought back warm feelings, similar to what she felt for him when she used to go to Brookdale. Zee looked at her journal and grabbed her pen, and wrote down the first thing she thought of.

I wonder if he's thinking about me right now.

6

BIG BROTHER RETURNS

Zee heard voices chatting in the living room. The twins started squealing excitedly, and Zee recognized that raspy voice over the commotion. She came out of her room to greet the newest visitor to their Malibu rental.

In the kitchen, she saw her parents and someone she had not seen since the summer. The tall, lanky figure turned toward her. "What's up, Zee?" Adam, her older brother, said.

"Ohmylanta!" Zee cried. "You made it!" She reached toward him for a hug.

"Yeah, didn't hit that much traffic on the PCH," Adam said. "You're getting tall, kid. What are they feeding you at boarding school?"

"Very funny, big brother," Zee said, happy to see her older sibling. "How long are you staying?"

"Until New Year's."

"Great," Zee said. "Plenty of time to crack jokes."

Adam reached for his bags and gathered them on his shoulders. "Where's my room? Naturally I'll take the biggest one, right?"

"Actually, Zee snagged it when we got here," Mr. Carmichael said. "Plenty of other rooms to choose from."

"Finders, keepers, bro," Zee said. "The one above me is just as big though. And with just as nice a view of the pool."

Adam started up the stairs toward the bedrooms, carrying his bags and texting on his phone as he walked. Zee followed him. She hadn't seen her big brother for months—Adam had left for Stanford right before the rest of the family moved to London. Though dealing with Adam's dirty laundry all over the house, his constant teasing, and his obsession with karate movies had annoyed Zee, she missed having him around every day. *Adam being back for the holidays makes things feel more like home,* she thought.

Adam stepped into a big bedroom and tossed his bag on the bed.

"Want to go for a swim?" Zee asked him. "The pool's heated."

Adam looked out the window at the pool. "Yeah, that does look like a good time. Let me unpack a few things and then I'll meet you out there."

• • •

The sun was bright and high in the sky when the two siblings got to the pool together, catching up on life since they'd been living apart. They laid out their towels on lounge chairs, sat back, kicked their feet up, and reclined.

"How's Stanford?" Zee asked.

"Good," Adam answered. "Classes are super hard. People are great. Fun times. How's boarding school? You get lonely?"

"At times. But I get to do my music every day, so that's fun."

"Yeah? I heard you're doing well there. That's what Mom said. You performed in a talent show, right?"

"The annual Creative Arts Festival," Zee said with a nod. "That was fun! I was in the school paper and everything. Made a few new friends afterwards. Music's good. Wish I could say the same about my grades."

"What?" Adam looked at her. "What's up with your grades?"

Zee looked around to see if her parents were within earshot. Then she leaned closer toward her brother. "Classes are harder. And, I dunno, with the move and stuff, it hasn't been easy to adjust. I'm seeing a therapist at school now."

"You are?"

"Since October."

"I had no idea."

"Yeah, it's been a thing. And she thinks I might have ADHD."

Adam turned his head quickly to Zee, his eyebrows arching upward. "Whoa," he said. "Wait, why? Are you disrupting class or something?"

"No, no," Zee said, again looking around for her parents. "But I do get nervous in class, and I get distracted and stuff, so they're doing a bunch of tests on me."

Adam turned his entire body toward Zee. "When I first started college, it was a huge transition for me too," he said, sitting up in his lounge chair. "I'd never lived away from home. And I remember having a few sleepless nights stressing out over classes and homework. But by the second semester, it got a lot better. Probably because I'd made friends and knew what to expect by then. Maybe when you go back to school, you'll feel a bit better."

Zee looked up at the blue sky and sighed. "I don't know, they make it sound like this has been an issue for some time."

"Well, has it?" Adam asked.

"I don't know," Zee said. She sat up in her lounge chair and turned toward Adam, crossing her legs. "But it felt good to go back to Brookdale with Chloe the other day. I saw my old friends and sat in on music class. And I invited them all over here for a jam session, which Mom has now turned into a holiday jamboree."

"We're having a holiday party?" Adam looked surprised.

"Yeah," Zee said, rolling her eyes. "A big one. You might as well invite your friends too, because it's going to be a big bash."

"All right, Mom! There is one guest I'll make sure to invite," he said, smoothing his hair back.

"Who?" Zee asked.

"Gabriella," Adam said.

Zee cocked her head to one side. "Who's Gabriella?"

"My girlfriend," Adam declared. "We've been dating since the beginning of the semester. She's super cool and her family lives around here. I was going to have her meet Mom and Dad for the first time over break."

Zee jerked her head back. "Wow, Adam, a girlfriend? A real, live girl?"

"What, you think she's made up or something? Yes, a real, live girl, Zee!"

Zee rolled her eyes, then smiled at her brother. "That's, uh, cool. Do Mom and Dad know?"

"They know I've been seeing someone, but they don't know all the details."

Zee leaned back in her lounge chair and sighed. "Well, at least they know more about your love life than mine."

Adam raised his eyebrows. "You have a love life, Zee? You're thirteen!"

"Yeah, and I have, like, a life," Zee said. "And an ex-boyfriend."

"An *ex-boyfriend!*" Adam laughed. "An ex means you had a *real* boyfriend. When did you have time to have a boyfriend? Who was he?"

"Hey there, romance police! Am I not allowed to have a boyfriend?"

Adam crossed his arms. "Well, eighth grade is a bit young to have a serious relationship."

"That's year nine in the U.K.," Zee said. "But don't get your knickers twisters, we broke it off after a week."

"Good thing," Adam said. "I don't need any guys trying to get with my little sister this early. And I didn't even meet this guy! Good thing you two broke up before I had a chance to really cross-examine him." He wrung his hands together and looked pensive, perhaps imagining himself giving the third degree to some poor unsuspecting guy who dared ask out his little sister. Zee looked at her brother, one eyebrow raised.

"Yes indeed," Zee said, letting out a chuckle. "A good thing for the both of us."

ICE CREAM SOCIAL

7

Zee

Girls. Maje news. Landon wants to get ice cream today at Jeni's. I'm going. It's either going to be awesome or awkward. My money's on awkward.

Chloe

WHAAAA?! When did this happen? When are you going? What are you wearing?

Ally

Zee

He asked me after I went to school with you, Chlo. Meeting this afternoon. I'm wearing denim shorts and a hoodie. Super casual. Because it's a casual meeting... right? What do you think he wants to talk about?

Ally

What did he say he wanted to talk about?

Zee

He said he wanted to catch up.

Chloe

Hmm… OK. Keep it casual. And super general. Tell him nothing about Archie! Keep it cool.

Zee

Right. RIGHT! Oy. I don't need anything else making this holiday complicated. Wish me luck.

The doorbell to the front door of the house rang loudly, so Zee put down her phone and went to the foyer. When Zee walked through the living room, she saw Mrs. Carmichael standing at the door with a crew of what looked like Santa's elves holding stockings, Christmas lights, wrapping paper, and red and green candles.

"Who are they?" Zee asked. "And what is going on?"

"These are the people who are going to get this place holiday ready!" Mrs. Carmichael said eagerly. "While we're in Brookdale, they are going to decorate the entire house."

"But I thought we were going to decorate the house," Zee said.

"Oh, we can do the tree if you like, dear," Mrs. Carmichael said. "But their job is to do all of the lights and decorating that would take us hours. We can use that free time to go shopping. Or, in your case, see an old friend. Let's go."

Zee watched the decorators quickly move through the house. She counted the number of people shuffling through the door with lights and knick-knacks. *Four... five... six? Why do we need all these people arranging our holiday?!* Zee blinked and twisted her head around, trying to keep up with the decorators who seemed to know exactly where things should be in the Carmichaels' temporary rental. She felt a lump in her throat. *Having someone else put up your Christmas stuff is just so... not festive.*

Mrs. Carmichael urged Zee out the house and into the car. They drove off toward the highway on two different missions: Zee was going to meet Landon after school at Jeni's, and Mrs. Carmichael was going to pop into some shops to pick up "a few things" for the party, "like snow cones and other decorations and two more Christmas trees."

"But Mom, we already have a tree in the dining room," Zee said.

"We need a few more," Mrs. Carmichael said, "for ambiance."

That ambiance is deforesting the California countryside. Can we at least get fake trees? Zee wondered to herself.

• • •

Jeni's Ice Creams was located just a few minutes away from Brookdale Academy, close enough that Landon, or any Brookdale student, could ride there on a bike. Zee twisted her hands nervously as they got closer.

Zee had tried to smooth things over with him before she

left by writing a heartfelt note, which she stuck in his backpack on their last day of school, but she never mentioned it to him directly. She had no idea if he had even read it. Even if he had, she knew the note wasn't enough to mend their friendship. Perhaps ice cream at Jeni's would help.

The ice cream shop was located in the same complex as Home and Hearts, where Mrs. Carmichael was eager to get holiday decorations. Zee and her mother walked into the ice cream parlor and took a seat near the front. A few minutes later, Landon rolled up on his bicycle and parked the bike next to the front entrance.

Zee smiled awkwardly at him as he walked over. "No detention today?" she cracked.

"Funny, Zee," Landon said with a smile. "Hi, Mrs. Carmichael."

"Hi, Landon," Mrs. Carmichael replied. "Nice to see you. I'm going to leave you here, Zee. I've got some shopping to do. Be back in about an hour? Text me if you're ready before then."

"Okay, Mom," Zee said. "We'll be here."

Mrs. Carmichael left Landon and Zee there, staring at the menu of ice cream flavors. "I think the mint chip is calling me," Zee said.

"The flavors haven't changed since you left," Landon replied.

"Awesome," Zee said. "What's cracking at school today?"

"Nothing. Same stuff. Can't wait to be on break in a few days."

"I know that feeling. Were classes harder this semester?"

"No harder than usual," Landon said. "I didn't have any distractions this semester."

Is he calling me a distraction? Zee wondered. *Did I actually give him a reason to lose his concentration? Did he think about me in class? Does he dream about me? Oh my gosh, if he still has feelings for me, this could be awkward!*

The two looked at the Crayola-colored flavors on display in the ice cream freezer. An employee behind the counter greeted them. "How can I help you?"

"She'll have a green mint chip," Landon said, ordering for Zee. "And I'll have a butter almond brittle. In waffle cones, please." Landon scooted toward the cash register.

How sweet of him to order for me, Zee thought. *This reminds me of how Archie used to do at our meetups at Moe's.*

"So, what's up for break?" Landon asked. "Got big plans?"

"Well, we're having the party at the house this weekend, as I announced in class the other day. My mom invited everyone's parents to join too."

"Yeah? It's a big to-do?" Landon asked, walking farther down the ice cream counter toward the cashier.

"I guess, like a big holiday barbecue," Zee said. "Food, decorations, big ol' tree. Music! And all The Beans members are coming so we can jam. You've gotta come."

"Sounds fun," Landon said. "I'll ask my parents."

"Here you go," the woman behind the counter said, passing two waffle cones to Landon and Zee.

Zee's eyes widened at the huge scoop of mint green with bits of chocolate sprinkled on top. "This looks heavenly."

Landon paid for the cones and followed Zee out the front door and toward a picnic table set up in the front of the shop. They sat down across from each other, eager to dive into their desserts. The air was crisp and the sun warmed their faces, almost threatening to melt their ice cream if they didn't eat it fast enough.

"Mm, just like I remembered," Zee said happily.

"How is it being back in town?" Landon asked.

"It's nice to be back in Brookdale," Zee said. "So many recognizable faces, places, my teachers, my friends. Old places I used to go. It's just really great."

"Nice," Landon said. "You see your old house yet?"

"No! Have you?"

"Yeah," Landon said, taking a lick of his ice cream. "I went by it a few times since you've been gone. Nice family lives there now. I rode by on my bike thinking about you."

Surprised, Zee took a pause from her ice cream. "Really? You thought about me enough to go by my old house?"

"Well, I was... uh... in the neighborhood," he said.

"Uh-huh," Zee said. "Why were you on my block?"

"Well, I have friends on that block too."

"Like who?"

"Like... um..." Landon hurriedly ate more ice cream.

"Yeah, right," Zee said. "Anyway."

"Anyway," Landon said. An awkward pause fell between them. Zee looked at the edge of the table in between bites, avoiding Landon's eyes until he finally changed the subject. "How's life in London? What's boarding school like?"

"It's all right," Zee said, nodding her head, still looking at her ice cream. "It's so weird not to sleep at home every night. But I got used to it. My roommate is a ballet dancer. And I met some cool friends. Jasper's there, you remember Jasper?"

"Ah, yeah, Jasper Chapman," Landon replied. "So, you and Jasper hang out?"

"Yeah. He helped me arrange my first song that I performed at our local talent show. My friend Archie helped me arrange some music for it."

"Archie?" Landon asked.

"Yeah," she stammered. Zee was hesitant to tell Landon more about him. She didn't really know her status with Archie, nor did she know her status with Landon, and she didn't want to confuse her status with either one of them any more than she already had. So she kept it vague. "I just met him on campus, which is pretty small, and the music circles are even smaller. So, people who have the same arts concentration tend to know each other."

"I see," Landon said, slowly nodding. "Cool."

"What's up with you?" Zee asked quickly, eager to change the subject.

"You know, chill. Still playing in the band with everyone."

"Including Kathi," Zee said.

"Unfortunately."

Zee smiled at this revelation. "Well, come to the party at my house this weekend, then we can jam together again.

Maybe we can stuff her in a bathroom or something while we play," she joked.

"Ha! That'd be fun!" Landon said.

They two ate their cones smiling and laughing while taking in the sights of people walking in and out of the mall stores. Zee began feeling more comfortable with Landon. She felt a burst of courage to try and explain herself and how she had left things with him. "So, Landon, I really wanted to ask..."

Just then, Zee's phone buzzed. She reached for it thinking that it was her mother, but was pleasantly surprised to see her pal Izzy Matthews video calling from London. Zee picked up the phone quickly. "It's my friend from The Hollows calling to say hi," Zee explained to Landon. She turned back to the phone. "Izzy!"

"Zee!" Izzy excitedly exclaimed. "How are you?"

"Good! I'm just here having ice cream at my favorite place," Zee said. She turned her phone around so Izzy could get a view of the street on a beautiful winter day in Southern California. Zee panned her phone around with her arms extended, rotating her body 360 degrees so she could show Izzy the palm trees, the sunny skies, people walking around in short sleeves and cutoff jeans, and the front door of Jeni's. Then she panned the camera toward Landon, who continued eating his ice cream and gave a polite wave. Izzy waved back, her eyes widening at the handsome guy by Zee's side. "What's up with you? How are things?" Zee asked.

"It's rather cold and dreary here in London, but it feels very much like Christmas and that feels good," Izzy said, stretching her neck as if trying to get a second look at Landon. "Looks like you've got some company there!"

"Yeah, I'm here with my friend Landon. Can I give you buzz later? I'll send you some photos of California."

"Right! Enjoy yourself," Izzy said as she slowly nodded and smiled. "And yes, definitely send some pics!"

Zee hung up the phone and turned to Landon. "Sorry about that," Zee said. "That was my friend Izzy. She's a YouTube star and everything is content for her."

"No worries. You guys friends?"

"Yeah, we met in the dorms."

Landon finished his cone and leaned forward with one elbow on the table. "I see your mom is a big social media star too," he said. "You're, like surrounded by celebrities. How California of you."

"Har har, Landon. That's hardly true," Zee said.

Just then, Mrs. Carmichael walked up to the picnic table where they were sitting. She had two large bags in her hand, presumably full of party goods. "Zee, I'm going to put these in the car and then we should head back, okay?"

"Sure," Zee said. She looked at Landon. "Guess my time is up. This was fun."

"Yeah," Landon said, standing up. He smiled sheepishly, then looked down at the table between them.

"Listen, come to the party and we can catch up more there," Zee said.

"Yeah," he said, tilting his head upward, smiling at Zee. "Good talk today."

"Yeah, it was."

Landon tossed his spare napkins into the trash and moved toward his bicycle. Zee watched his every move, trying to hide her smile from him, secretly hoping he really would show up to her house this weekend for the party. Mrs. Carmichael closed the trunk of her car and walked toward the two. "Ready, Zee? Good to see you, Landon."

"Bye, Mrs. Carmichael," he replied. He turned to Zee and winked.

Zee stood on the curb, watching as he biked down the street and away from her. She bit her lower lip. *That wasn't too bad*, she thought. *He's still funny. He's still cool. He's still... cute. Cuter than I remember.*

She turned toward the car and saw her mother standing there with a wide-eyed smile on her face. "So, was that a nice visit?" Mrs. Carmichael asked.

"Yeah," Zee said, feeling a flutter in her chest. "Just like old times."

8

OVER THE TOP

*T*he decorations Mrs. Carmichael bought at Home and Hearts were just the tip of the iceberg of holiday decor at their Malibu rental. When Zee and her mother returned from shopping, they found the entire house, including the oversized aluminum tree set up in the space near the dining area Zee picked out earlier, completely decked out. White and green garlands wrapped around the staircase and awnings, and fairy lights twinkled around window trimmings and fireplaces. Snowman figurines and reindeer antlers were perched on mantels and bookshelves.

"Festive chic!" Mrs. Carmichael declared when she walked in the house.

Zee looked around wide-eyed, but her shoulders slumped forward and her mouth suddenly had a sour taste in it. "I thought we would decorate the house together, as a family," Zee said. "I was looking forward to putting ornaments on the tree."

"You still can, honey," Mrs. Carmichael said. "Look, they left plenty of room on the tree for some tinsel."

"We have other people decking our halls," Zee said. "That's not how I thought Christmas would go." The house looked like it was straight out of a West Elm catalog. "Where are the homemade decorations we had on our old tree, the ones I made when I was in kindergarten?"

"They're packed away at home in London, honey," Mrs. Carmichael said. "I'm sorry I didn't think to bring them, but I knew we were having professionals do everything this year."

Mrs. Carmichael took out her phone and dialed a number, pacing around the living room as she waited for someone to answer the call. "Hi, how are you? Great, great. Yes, we need catering for about fifty people. What sort of things do you do for a party that size? Yes, at a house in Malibu.... Mm-hmm, yes... Right... Sounds delicious!"

Zee couldn't believe it. Catering? Zee was used to her mom making all the holiday treats. *Is she really going to have other people bake her famous Christmas almond crescent cookies?* Zee thought. *Does that mean we won't bake Christmas cookies together this year?*

"Zee, is anyone in your class allergic to nuts? There are a few vegetarians, right? We should have options," Mrs. Carmichael said before she turned back to the phone. "Excuse me, no nuts in anything, please."

"But I like nuts," Zee said just as Mrs. Carmichael hung up with the caterer.

"Yes, but we can't risk anyone getting sick at the event. I mean, it will be online!" her mother said. "Oh, and let's discuss what you're wearing. Shall we get you a new outfit? So we can coordinate?"

"I was thinking of a holiday T-shirt and jeans, since this

is California and it's seventy degrees out. That's what I'll be comfortable in."

Mrs. Carmichael shook her head. "Where's your holiday spirit?"

"The T-shirt is red and green!" Zee said. She couldn't take it anymore. She felt frustration bubbling up in her throat. She just wanted a regular family holiday at home, with a tree filled with homemade decorations and cookies and her mother focused on her family, not her followers on Instagram. Zee felt a pit in her stomach. Anger seethed from her belly and rose up to her throbbing temples.

"What else, Mom?!" Zee blurted out, unable to control the disappointment any longer. "Can I only watch the approved holiday movies? The ones that are on brand with your social media presence? Am I allowed to drink hot chocolate out of my favorite holiday mug for fear it won't match the couch? Is this a family holiday or outtakes from The Grove holiday ad?"

Mrs. Carmichael's smile faded as her mouth formed a tight, horizontal line. Zee knew she had upset her mother. But before her mom could say anything, Zee ran off to her room, brushing past her father on the way.

Surprised, Mr. Carmichael looked at his wife and saw her standing in the middle of the living room, her head in her hands, trying to wipe tears away from her face without anyone seeing her. Then he turned on his heels and followed his daughter.

Zee turned quickly into her room and shut the door. She looked around and noticed that everything she'd put there was still in its place. The Christmas decorators hadn't touched her room. *Thank goodness*, she thought, rolling her eyes. Zee plopped down on her bed, regretting how she had snapped at her mother. She looked over at the nightstand by her bed and reached for her journal under the lamp. Picking up a pen, she began writing:

I feel like my version of the holidays has been erased for the Instagram version. Fake snow, fake decorations, fake holiday cheer. Everything is store-bought and same-day delivered. Not one imperfect holiday decoration allowed! Mom, why is everything all about looking perfect for social media? What about the real version of our holiday?

Zee flipped back a few pages in her journal and found the holiday song she'd been writing. She started humming the melody as she read the words. The lyrics sparked memories of the happy Christmases of her youth. Her mother and her making cookies all day. Her family walking around the neighborhood to check out the Christmas lights. Zee making holiday decorations at school, including the handprint in plaster when she was in kindergarten that Mrs. Carmichael had saved and put on the tree for the last six years. And all the fun Zee had making forts and homemade decorations with Chloe and Ally. Zee thought about that time she and Chloe tried to find Santa in their subdivision. They had set up a camera on Chloe's roof to attempt to catch him in the act (no such luck). Even as Zee got older and outgrew some things, like taking a photo on Santa's lap, she still wanted to watch her twin siblings grow up and participate in the same holiday traditions she used to have.

Zee wrote a few more lines down in the journal:

I don't need fancy gifts, big toys or trains,
Just wanna eat Christmas cookies near the fire again
With you… with you….

Zee flopped back onto her bed. She threw her arms over her face. With this holiday party her mother was planning, it seemed that the family Christmases she was used to were things of the past. "Christmas has been outsourced," Zee said out loud, sighing heavily.

Mr. Carmichael knocked on Zee's door, then pushed it open wide enough for him to see her splayed out on her bed. "Uh, what was that about?" he said.

"Nothing, Dad," Zee said, shoving her face into a pillow.

"Nothing? That was definitely something. You left your mother practically in tears in our living room," he said. Zee could tell from his tone of voice that she was in trouble. "You can't talk to your mother like that."

"I know. I'm sorry, Dad," Zee said. She didn't move from her bed. Zee kept her face embedded in the pillow, fighting back tears. Her father put his hand on her shoulder, nudging her to turn over and sit up.

"What's gotten into you?" Mr. Carmichael said. "I thought you'd be happy as a clam being back here for the holidays with all your old friends."

"I *am* happy," Zee said. "But I also miss the old things."

"What old things?"

"*My* old things! My decorations! My tree! My old house! My mom! There're just so many other people here. Like, I wanted to decorate my own tree! And where are all our decorations? It's just not the same."

"I see," Mr. Carmichael said, nodding slowly. He listened as he processed what Zee was feeling: out of her element in her own home, even on the holidays. "When you were young, I remember your mother hand painting porcelain decorations for the tree. Making homemade cookies for the neighbors, then going to your school holiday bake sale and manning the cash register to sell goods for your school band. Same thing with Adam—she knitted Christmas hats for him for years. Your mother does not do anything halfway. That is especially true for the holidays."

"But I loved helping her with those things," Zee said, "and now it seems like my help isn't good enough."

"That's not true, Zee," Mr. Carmichael said. "She always loves it when you help her! You can still decorate a tree if you want. Why don't you talk to your mother and tell her how you feel?"

"Because she doesn't care!" Zee exclaimed. "She only cares about taking beautiful photos for Instagram and having everything look perfect!"

"Now that's not true, Zee. I know for a fact she was planning to bake cookies with you and the twins because she mentioned it when she told Camilla to buy extra flour and eggs at the grocery store the other day."

"Well, I don't feel like she cares about spending the holidays with me."

Mr. Carmichael sat beside her on the bed. "Zee, your mother has looked forward to Christmas for two months. She wanted all of us—your brother and Camilla included—together in California having the best holiday possible. That's why she rented this huge house here! That's why she's decorating the house like mad with a professional team."

"But I don't *want* professional!"

Mr. Carmichael looked out the door across from Zee's room to the backyard. He could see his wife talking to the gardener as they gestured at the grounds. A moment passed and the gardener went back to work. Then Mrs. Carmichael looked out over the beach and put her hand to her forehead, as if she knew that she had somehow done something wrong. It was the first time that Mr. Carmichael saw his wife look so sad around Christmas.

He turned to Zee. "Your mother didn't think this Instagram thing was going to be a big deal at first. She started taking some cute photos of herself with the twins and putting them on social media mainly to follow you, but then a lot of people liked the photos, and boom—it took off. So she turned it into a business for herself. You should be proud!"

Zee wiped her nose and looked down at her feet.

Mr. Carmichael continued. "This is the first thing your

mother has had for herself since you were a little girl. Actually, since before you were born. Your mom gave up her career to raise you and your brother. After you started going to school, she went back to work, thinking she'd have her career again. Then the twins arrived, and she was at home with kids again. She has given her all to us. And now, seeing how she can turn time with her family into an actual business has been quite satisfying for her. It's made her very happy."

"I know," Zee said, "and I am proud of her. I just wish that she can focus less on social media and more on just us."

Mr. Carmichael put his arm around his daughter. "You should tell her how you feel. Maybe you two can go out to dinner or something and have some quality time. I'm sure she'd love to have an outing with you without having to shop for a party or create any Instagram content."

Zee looked out the door at her mother, who was now pacing the perimeter of their backyard. Zee could tell she was thinking. Maybe thinking about her. Maybe thinking about how she can get this holiday back on track with her daughter. Feeling guilty watching her mother worry, Zee turned back to her father.

"I guess I was the one who invited the entire eighth grade class to our house for a holiday party," Zee said. "You're right, I'll talk to her."

9

A NEW APPROACH

Zee took a big breath in and closed her eyes. She knew what she had to do.

She walked into the living room where her mother was studying the decorations, taking in the work by the professional elves she hired to do the job. Mrs. Carmichael had just hung up the phone with a company that would fill their backyard with fake snow and sled runs for the party, and another company that would bring a snow cone machine. The food had been ordered and the goody bags were almost all set. Mrs. Carmichael looked at her phone and pulled up a checklist. She'd taken care of most of her party planning to-do list.

Zee looked at her mother. Mrs. Carmichael was wearing a plaid wrap skirt and wedge heels, and her hair was elegantly styled. *Wow, she does look like a regal Mrs. Claus*, Zee thought. She smiled, though her mother couldn't see her.

Then Zee looked at the decorations around the living room. The candles added warm flickers of light. Seven hand-sewn stockings, including one for Camilla, were hung around the fireplace. In addition to the main tree in the dining area, there was a small white Christmas tree in the corner near the coffee machine. And, to Zee's surprise, there were also some personal items—small family photos were placed on the kitchen counter and the fireplace mantle so that the house felt a little more like home.

"That's a nice touch," Zee said out loud.

"Thanks," Mrs. Carmichael said. "I put those there myself."

"I know," Zee said, walking closer to her mother. "I'm sorry for what I said. I'm sorry I hurt your feelings. I'm sorry I'm a horrible daughter."

Mrs. Carmichael let out a gentle laugh. "Well, hold on. I accept your apology, but you're not a horrible daughter. I get why you were feeling the way you did."

Zee hugged her mother's waist. Mrs. Carmichael hugged her back, kissing her forehead. "Listen, this whole Christmas is for you—and your siblings, but really for you. I wanted to give you the best Christmas you'd ever seen. I want this house to feel like our home, hence all the decorations," Mrs. Carmichael said.

"Really?" Zee asked. "It's not just for Instagram?"

Mrs. Carmichael rolled her eyes. "Yes, I do have to film content during the holidays because a few brands are paying me to. But that's the business of being an influencer."

"I get it, but I'm not just one of your 15,000 followers," Zee said. "I just want to drink hot chocolate by the pool. But are you gonna be too busy for that?"

"Please," Mrs. Carmichael said with a wave of her hand. "I would never be too busy for hot chocolate with you." She looked around the home. Everything was in its place. Looking down at her watch, she saw it was 6:30 p.m. and got an idea. "Grab your shoes. Let's go out for a bit."

"Isn't it almost dinnertime?" Zee asked.

"Yes, but tonight we can do dinner by ourselves. Just the two of us, so we can sit and talk and catch up. Camilla already made the twins dinner, and your dad and Adam can eat on their own."

Zee looked surprised at her mother's impulsive idea but was eager to spend quality time alone with her. So Zee nodded and went to her room to find her purse, fix her hair, and grab her shoes. Then mother and daughter got into their car and drove toward town.

• • •

The two arrived at one of their favorite restaurants, Milly's, and settled into a comfortable back booth. The smell of simmering onions and garlic butter permeated the main dining room. Zee reviewed the menu eagerly. "I think we should get some spinach dip for sure," she said.

After the server came and took their order, Zee and her mom leaned toward each other. "So, do you like being back?" Mrs. Carmichael asked.

"Of course, Mom."

"It's not exactly Brookdale, I get it."

"True, but it's closer to home than life in London. At least here I can remember which side of the street cars drive on. And eat decent tacos."

"Right," Mrs. Carmichael said. "So tell me, how was your visit with Landon? Seems you had a good time."

"Yeah, he's still the same. I'm hoping he comes to the party."

"Speaking of boys," Mrs. Carmichael said, her voice dropping an octave, "you've mentioned somebody named Archie a few times back in London. Who is Archie? Was he like, you know, someone special?"

Zee froze. She did not want to explain her short romance with Archie, not over dinner and not, well, maybe ever. "*Mo-ooooom!*"

"I just thought I'd ask. His name did come up several times, but there was no real explanation as to who he was."

How can I get around having to go deep about Archie? Zee thought wildly. *Talk fast and change the subject!* "Archie Saint John. Year nine. From London. Rich kid. Great guitar player. Super nice, and that's it," Zee said.

The server came over with the spinach dip, and Zee eagerly grabbed a chip and spooned herself a bite. "This is *sooo* good," she said, trying to move on to another subject.

"Fine," Mrs. Carmichael said. "I'll leave it be for now, but I'm going to come back to it. In other news, any word on who is coming to this party on Saturday? I'm going to start assembling gift bags, so I need to know how many pairs of pajamas to buy."

Zee took another chip and chewed furiously. "Mom, don't you think that's a bit much? To buy pajamas for the entire eighth grade class and their parents?"

"But this is a holiday bash! It's a generous time of the year. I can't ask people to drive from L.A. to Malibu and not gift them well."

Zee put her chip down. It was her opportunity to come clean about her mom's behavior. "Mom, do you think you're going a bit overboard?"

"What do you mean?" Mrs. Carmichael asked.

"It's just... I remember when we used to recycle magazines and newspapers to use as gift wrap, and we used to make homemade body scrubs and fruit tarts as gifts. Now we're giving people designer candles and tote bags?"

Mrs. Carmichael tilted her head as she considered this criticism. "But I bought all of the produce for the event from local farmers. And the candles are locally sourced too."

"Yeah, from Fred Segal!" Zee said.

"Well, I wanted something a bit more upscale for this party, honey. Being that it will be on social media and all."

Zee leaned back in her seat. "Ever since I was little, you taught me to be being mindful about spending and trying to recycle where possible. And our school—heck, our whole town is all about saving the earth and eco-friendly stuff. The holiday decorations and over-the-top gift bags are so not on

brand for Brookdale. What are parents going to think when they show up and see this ridiculously lavish party?"

Mrs. Carmichael looked at her daughter. She took out her phone and pulled up photos from the house. The house looked amazing, with the reindeer figures and poinsettias perfectly placed around the living space. But only half of the decorations were visible since Mrs. Carmichael had been more focused on taking close-ups of the twins and Adam and Zee in the photos. "Maybe I could cut back on some of the holiday trimmings," Mrs. Carmichael said.

"Ya think?" Zee asked.

"All right, you win," Mrs. Carmichael responded. "Let's see how we can be more mindful about the decorations. Maybe I shouldn't get the gold flakes for the snack table."

"That's a start," Zee said. "And can we incorporate some earth-friendly stuff into the party? Like biodegradable cutlery?"

"Good idea."

Zee was full of ideas. "And cut the candles. Too expensive. And the bags need to be swapped for recycled totes. And I guess you can keep the pajamas, like you did for our sleepover in Notting Hill with Izzy, Jameela, and Ally. But maybe look at a sustainable brand of PJs? Like ones that use recycled cotton?"

"Got it," Mrs. Carmichael said. "Can we still keep the snow machine? It really will give the place that winter wonderland feel."

"But how much gas is needed to create fake snow? It'll be like a semi-truck idling in our backyard for three hours."

"Let's discuss it," Mrs. Carmichael said. "Maybe we can rent a machine to create flurries, but not a blizzard."

The two continued to brainstorm ways to create an eco-friendly winter wonderland. Out went the candles, balloons, and fancy designer gift bags, and in came the recyclable totes stamped with small Christmas trees and the date of the party. No gold-flaked cupcakes for the desserts, but Mrs. Carmichael agreed to buy Beyond Meat meatballs. "Does that sound more like Brookdale?" Mrs. Carmichael asked.

"Absolutely!" Zee said, smiling as she looked at her mom. "Oh, one more thing—don't forget the hot chocolate!"

10

PARTY TIME

On Saturday morning, the day of the party, the house was bustling with activity. The caterer and party staffers arrived to put the finishing touches on decorating the house, and Zee woke up early to help her mother oversee the setup. "This is your party too, and you helped pick out the decor," Mrs. Carmichael had said. "You should have as much input on the decorations as I do."

The outdoor patio area looked like an actual winter wonderland. Zee agreed with her mother that having fake snow on the ground would give the party that extra degree of specialness. Snow gently fell from a small snow machine bolted to the gazebo roof, and the snowmakers constructed two sled ramps at the far end of the yard—one tall and steep for the bigger kids, and another one less steep for the twins. "That was my idea," Zee said to herself.

The pool had large plastic—and reusable—snow globes that floated on top of the water, and matching small, recycled plastic globes at the snack table. The Christmas trees outside were all aluminum. "No trees were harmed in the making of the backyard decor, Zee," Mrs. Carmichael assured her.

A hot chocolate, frozen hot chocolate, and s'mores station was set up near the firepit, and the party staffers put plaid blankets on the chairs around it. It was supposed to be a warm day in the mid-seventies in Malibu, but the blankets were a nice touch anyway.

"This all looks great," Zee said with a satisfied nod. "Where are the gift bags?"

"In the foyer, sweetie, so people can grab them on the way out," Mrs. Carmichael said as she adjusted an ornament on the tree.

Zee went to the front of the house and peeked inside one of the bags. Even those were mindfully assembled—homemade cookie mixes and hot chocolate, as well as the pajamas, all tucked into reusable totes.

"Mom, you really did act on my suggestions," Zee said. "I'm surprised."

"Things still look chic," Mrs. Carmichael said with a smile. "And now they're more on brand with Brookdale."

• • •

Zee heard excited chatter from the front of the house. Her mother was laughing and swooning over something, and Adam and her father were huddled together. Then there was another female voice, a sweet, cheerful one interspersed with giggles. Zee walked toward the front entrance and saw her family talking and smiling with a woman Zee had never seen before. Adam spotted his sister standing at the end of the foyer and called her over. "Zee, come here, I want to introduce you."

He turned to the beautiful young woman with long dark hair and dark features standing next to him. She wore a festive red maxi dress. "Zee, this is Gabriella, my girlfriend," Adam said.

Whoa, Zee thought.

Gabriella smiled broadly. "Hi, Zee. Adam talks about you all the time. Nice to meet you finally."

"Hi," Zee said. "Really?"

"Yeah, he says you're a very talented musician. He showed me the video clip of you performing at school recently and everything."

"Wow, Adam," Zee said. "I didn't know you followed my music career."

He shrugged. "Can't help but follow it. Mom and Dad always brag about you to everyone."

"You follow Zee without me telling you what's going on, don't lie," Mrs. Carmichael said with a grin. "Come on in, you two. Gabriella, there's a spare bedroom upstairs where you can put your things and freshen up."

"Where did you guys meet?" Zee asked as they walked through the house.

"We met in one of our pre-law classes together," Gabriella said.

Mr. Carmichael turned to his wife. Mrs. Carmichael turned to her husband. Then they both turned to Adam.

Mr. Carmichael spoke first. "Pre-law?"

"Yeah," Gabriella said. "The set of classes you take if you intend to go into law."

"As in, before you go to law school?" Mrs. Carmichael asked.

"Yes, Mom," Adam said. "I didn't tell you guys because I wanted to surprise you here."

The parents were in fact quite surprised at this news. "Why, Adam, that's awesome! I had no idea you wanted to be a lawyer," Mrs. Carmichael said.

"You see enough cool TV lawyers with great hair and sleek suits, and you get inspired," Adam joked. "Just kidding. I want to keep the good guys out of prison and the bad guys in. And I'd like to have my own practice someday."

"That's wonderful news, Adam!" Mrs. Carmichael said, hugging her son. "That's a gift Santa will have a hard time topping. C'mon, guys, let's get you settled before company comes!"

The Carmichaels ushered Gabriella and Adam toward the living room and asked one of the party staffers hired for the day to bring them some apple cider. "Let's have a toast to these two future lawyers!" Mr. Carmichael said. A server brought a round of champagne flutes filled with apple cider, and Mr. Carmichael gave a toast. "To your future!" he said excitedly.

Zee stood off to the side and watched her parents make a ceremony out of her brother's announcement and his new girlfriend. Mrs. Carmichael took photos of the two, then flipped her camera around and posed with her son, Gabriella, and her husband. "Worth the main page indeed," Mrs. Carmichael said, smiling at her phone.

· · ·

Zee texted Chloe and Ally, eagerly awaiting their arrival.

Zee

Ladies, when are you getting here?

Ally

Waiting on my auntie.

Chloe

Leaving now!

Zee

Good! Need backup. Adam's girlfriend is here.

Chloe

What do you need backup for? Is she mean?

Zee

No, not at all, she's pretty and nice.

Chloe

You'd expect anything less for your brother?

Zee

No, it's just she's sooo pretty. And smart. And my parents are, like, obsessed with her. So I'm now a weird third wheel here in my own house. I need company! Get to this party soon!

Chloe

We're on our way, girl.

11

A HAPPY REUNION

ee was waiting patiently by the door, checking her phone every now and then. Ally had texted her five minutes ago to say she was en route. This would finally be the reunion Zee had hoped for: Ally, Chloe, and her, all together in person for the first time since the summer. Zee really didn't care if anybody else showed up at this party so long as the three of them were together.

She paced back and forth in front of the window by the door and touched her nose up to the glass. *I wonder what Ally's wearing?* Zee thought to herself. *Is Ally going to be as well groomed as she was when she came to London?* Finally, the doorbell rang, and Zee sprinted to it. She flung the door open.

"Hiii!" Zee said, jumping up and down like a ping-pong ball on a table.

Ally stood at the door with a broad smile. Her hair fell around her face and was held back with a sparkly hairband, and she had on a black mini dress and black sandals with a few bangles. "Hi!" Ally said, giving Zee a hug. "Wow, look at this place! It's so... big! And look at the decorations!"

"Yeah, it's my mom's doing. Wait, where's *your* mom?"

"She was tied up," Ally said. "My aunt dropped me off. She had to jet, so she told me to tell your family thanks and happy holidays."

Zee blinked a few times, surprised that Ally's mom opted out of the party, but quickly refocused on Ally. "Come in! Come in! Come in! Everything is ready, Chloe's on her way, and then we can partaaayy!"

A party staffer offered to take Ally's bag, and Zee grabbed Ally by her free hand and tugged her toward the living room. "Once everyone leaves, you, me, and Chloe can watch holiday movies here. This couch is sooo comfortable. You are staying the night, right?"

"Um, I don't know. I have to ask my mom," Ally replied.

"But you should have asked before!" Zee said anxiously. "I asked you before to clear it with her! I have a whole plan!"

"I know, I just never got a chance to ask. I'll text her."

Riiing! Another buzz at the door. "Maybe that's Chloe!" Zee said, running to the door. Chloe had arrived with her parents and walked quickly through the foyer into the house to greet her friends.

"Hey, hey, hey! Allyyy!" Chloe said.

"Chloeee!" Ally screamed.

The three hugged as tightly as human beings could hug one another. They squealed so loudly that the twins waddled over toward the front door to see what was going on. "OMG, OMG, I'm so happy we're finally all back together again!" Zee said. "Let's take a selfie!"

The girls took photos of each other hugging and making

funny faces at the camera, then with their backs against one another, then kicking out their legs like the Rockettes, then giggling. "We are baaackk!" Chloe declared. "Ooh, girls, guess what? I brought pajamas! Candy cane–striped ones!"

"Wait," Zee said. "Are those the ones—"

Chloe nodded. "We decided to buy them together, remember? We saw them online and we said we had to have these for holiday photos. Ally, did you bring yours?"

Ally looked blankly at the girls. "No, I forgot," she said. "Sorry, there's been so much going on at home."

"That's okay," Chloe said, "because I brought an extra pair for you! Black Friday, baby! I went IN!"

Chloe tossed the PJs at Ally, who smiled and held on to them as the threesome made their way to the backyard. Chloe and Ally gazed at the decorations and food on display. "This looks amazing!" Ally said. "Look at the snow! Of course everything is picture perfect."

"Mom actually wanted to go over-the-top ridiculous, but I helped her create something more chill. You know, so we can celebrate but also not hurt the earth," Zee said.

"Right," said Chloe. "And wear matching PJs and get amazing photos and eat the most delicious cookies. Priorities, Zee."

"Is Santa coming?" Ally asked.

Ally and Chloe looked expectantly at Zee. Zee felt a pit in her stomach. *D'oh! Why didn't I get Santa to show up? How could I have a party without Santa? Great, now Ally's going to be totally disappointed and really never stay the night! Have I ruined this entire party?*

"I'm just kidding!" Ally said. "C'mon, let's check out the sled run."

• • •

Ring riiing riiiiing... The doorbell blared throughout the house as if someone were leaning on the button. It took no longer than three seconds for Camilla to open the door.

"Finally," a sour-faced thirteen-year-old said, peering around Camilla to see herself inside.

"Hi, I'm Mrs. Barney," Kathi's mom said politely. "Nice to meet you. Kathi, come and introduce yourself please."

Kathi looked quickly at Camilla and said, "Hi, I'm Kathi. Where's Zee?"

Camilla nodded to them both. "Zee's in the backyard. Please come in."

Just then, Mrs. Carmichael walked up to the front door. "Hi there, long time no see! Thank you, Camilla. I can take them myself."

Mrs. Carmichael walked Mrs. Barney and her daughter toward the back of the property, Kathi spinning her head left and right to take in every detail of the house along the way. "Ooh. Oh. Wow. Is this yours?" she said, pointing at every interesting artifact or decoration they walked past. "That looks expensive. Is that rented or is that yours?"

"Kathi!" her mother scolded her. "Just relax, you're not a reporter!"

"I just want to know what's, like, real," Kathi said.

"It's all real," Mrs. Carmichael said. "I know, right? This house seemed to come with everything."

Mrs. Carmichael walked the pair through the living room to the doors that opened to the backyard and pool. Kathi stopped in her tracks and took in the expansive backyard covered with snow and holiday goodies. "Wow," she said. "This is better than Disneyland."

"Thank you, Kathi," Mrs. Carmichael said. "Why don't you find Zee? I think she was with her friends by the gazebo."

Kathi's eyes wandered across the patio. She walked purposefully toward the gazebo and saw Zee, Chloe, and Ally singing and gabbing away like old pals. "The three amigas," Kathi said as she got closer to them.

Zee turned around as Chloe and Ally looked on. "Ahem," Zee said through pursed lips. "Kathi Barney. Welcome."

"Ally!" Kathi said excitedly. "How long's it been, like, two years?"

"A while," Ally replied. "How are you?"

"Same," Kathi said, leaning back and looking at Ally's complete holiday look from head to toe. "You look good. You're living in Paris now, right?"

"Yes, and thanks, Kathi. How nice of you to say."

Kathi looked back at Zee. "So, how's London, Zee? Have you seen Big Ben? The Palace? The Queen?"

"Nope, none of them," said Zee. "I go to school outside of London, so I spend most of my time in the countryside."

"Got it," Kathi said. "It must be awesome to live at school. Living away from your parents. No rules to follow. Getting to do what you want."

"Not exactly!" Zee said. "I have more rules at school than I do at home. And my roommate is a ballet dancer who wakes up before dawn and has a rigid schedule. She dances right up until dinner most nights."

"What's her name?"

"Jameela Chopra," Zee said.

"Is she nice?" Kathi asked.

"When she wants to be."

"Does she have a cool family?"

"Dunno, I've only seen her parents once or twice."

"Do you guys stay up late talking and watching movies?"

"Um, no," Zee said, turning her head to the side and wondering where this line of questioning about her roommate was headed. "She's in bed pretty early. I might stay up studying, but usually I fall asleep listening to music on my headphones."

"Does she sneak in fun snacks to your room?" Kathi asked.

"Um, not really?" Zee said. "But I keep a stash of candy in my nightstand."

"Wow," Kathi said. "She sounds like less fun than I do!"

Zee looked at Kathi. "Oh, don't worry, Kathi. I don't think anyone could ever be less fun than you."

Chloe and Ally giggled. "Ooh, *snap!*" Chloe said, cheering

on her friend Zee. Kathi stood still, smirking as the girls laughed. Zee cocked her head to one side, smiled, then turned on her heel and walked away toward the snack table.

• • •

Marcus Montgomery was going places. At least he wanted people to think he was going places. The budding entrepreneur prided himself on starting his own business trading sports memorabilia when he was eleven (with help from his older brother) and was eager to become a member of the Forbes 500 before he turned twenty-one. Now, Marcus ran a lawn mowing business called LawnCuts with his best friend Conrad Mitori. They even have custom company uniforms and their own lawn mowers. The duo also started a tutoring business for middle schoolers. When he wasn't running his empire, Marcus liked reading biographies of famous business leaders and constantly checked Yahoo Finance in his spare time.

Marcus's entrepreneurial ways made Chloe swoon, but of course she never told Marcus how she felt. Meanwhile, Marcus was more intrigued by Zee. He liked Zee's creativity and thought she could be a complementary creative right brain to his more practical left brain. He was all business, she was all fun.

Marcus was eager to catch up with Zee since seeing her at school earlier this week. He put on his crispest button-down collared shirt and a pair of sharply pressed dark-green slacks. His sneakers were fresh out of the box—he also collected sneakers and prided himself on having the most unique kicks of his friends. Marcus showed up with his parents and Conrad promptly at the start of the party with a nice wreath in hand as a gift. After ringing the doorbell, Marcus quickly spotted Mrs. Carmichael as she came out of the kitchen.

"Hi, Marcus! It's been a while!" she said.

"Greetings, Mrs. Carmichael," Marcus said. "Thanks for having us."

"Zee and the girls just went to the gazebo in the backyard. Why don't you join them there?"

Marcus straightened his posture and followed a staffer to the gazebo while Conrad looked for the snack table. Marcus's parents made polite conversation with Mrs. Carmichael.

Zee, Chloe, and Ally were still huddled together, making short videos on their phones and giggling about Kathi Barney's awkward social behaviors. Marcus, ever the polite gentleman, cleared his throat as he neared them. "Am I interrupting something?" he asked.

"No, you're not interrupting!" Chloe said eagerly. "It's so good to see you!"

Zee turned toward him. "Hey, Marcus! Wow, look at you!"

Marcus smiled, his cheeks growing round. "I'm in a holiday mood, what can I say? How are you? How're things in London? Or should I say, *cheerio!*"

"London's great," Zee said. "And I don't think I've said 'cheerio' to anyone, even in London, Marcus!"

Marcus looked intently at Zee before Chloe interrupted. "Can we get you something to drink? Some hot chocolate or something?" she asked him.

"Nah, I'm good," Marcus said, not breaking his gaze at Zee. "Wow, Zee, the house looks amazing."

"Thanks, I helped organize it," Zee said.

"You did?" Marcus asked, surprised.

"Yeah, the food, the decor, the gift bags. The biodegradable cups you're gonna sip a frozen chocolate out of. Want one?"

Marcus smiled and nodded, seemingly impressed by her attention to detail in addition to her creative spirit. "Yeah, I'll try one," he said. Zee handed him the drink. "So, what's up with boarding school? You still playing music there?"

"Yep," Zee said. "I just performed in our school's annual talent show on my own."

"You did a solo?" Marcus leaned back from her, looking impressed. "Look at you! It's like when Beyoncé broke out from Destiny's Child."

"Funny, Marcus. Not quite, but it was fun!"

Chloe tried to offer Marcus a snack. "Some brownies or some Christmas cookies?" she asked.

"I'm okay," he said politely again, quickly going back to Zee.

Zee turned to Chloe to try to include her in the conversation. "Chloe, how's soccer going?"

"Good! I scored two goals in the last game," she said proudly.

"Wow, Chloe! That's awesome," Ally said.

"Yup," Marcus said. "Nice work."

"I appreciate that, Marcus," Chloe said, her voice lowering an octave. Zee and Ally looked at each other, smirking. Marcus turned to Ally. "Ally, I haven't seen you in, like, two years. How's Pare-ee?"

"It's fine. It's very French," Ally said as Chloe walked off to grab some food.

"It's got to be a little more than that," Marcus said. "My parents always talk about going to Paris. I think they went there for their honeymoon. Everyone talks about Paris in love stories and stuff. What's so great about it?"

Ally rolled her eyes and smiled. "It is pretty romantic, I guess. Cute cafés, people walking slowly on the sidewalks hand in hand. You know, rom-com stuff. I write about some of it for my school journal. But I personally haven't done any of that. Yet."

Chloe came back from the kitchen. "Maybe you just haven't found the right person to do that stuff with," she said, putting snacks she got for Marcus down on the table in front of him, winking as she walked away.

Zee looked around her backyard. The party was getting into full swing. Music filled the house and kids flocked to the backyard, tossing snowballs at each other and sipping on hot chocolate. Some of the parents gathered with Mr. Carmichael by the barbecue grill, while Mrs. Carmichael strutted around the party greeting guests. Zee had her friends and they had smiles on their faces.

Strong start so far, Zee thought. *But I wonder if Landon's going to show up.*

12

A FESTIVE SINGALONG

The rest of Brookdale's eighth grade music class filed out onto the patio of the Carmichael's home, and the kids took turns enjoying the sled runs, the snowballs, and the holiday decorating station. Zee, Chloe, and Ally stuck together all evening, greeting their friends and swooning over stories Adam's girlfriend, Gabriella, told them about college.

"I wonder if I should play soccer at Stanford," Chloe said, thinking out loud. "How's the shopping? Where do you shop there?"

"I shop online," Gabriella said. "I get my stuff delivered to the dorm. It's fun to people-watch in the quad and check out what everyone's wearing. That's where I get a lot of my inspiration from."

Chloe and Ally were hanging on her every word. "Can we follow you on Instagram?" they asked.

Soon after, Mr. P arrived with his partner, greeting his students as he meandered through the house. "Mr. P, you made it!" Zee said once she spotted him. "You might be the only teacher I've ever had over before."

"Thanks, Zee, I'm honored," he replied.

Landon was the last to arrive at the massive holiday party. By then, the driveway and street around the house were completely full, so his parents drove to the end of the block to find a spot to park. Carrying a small bag with a box of chocolates he brought for Zee as a gift, Landon rang the doorbell and shifted from foot to foot, waiting nervously for someone to open the door.

Finally, a staffer opened the door for the family. The Becks stepped inside the foyer, looking around the main room for a recognizable face. Mr. Carmichael walked by and recognized Landon's father. "Hey, John, how are you? Been a while, huh?"

While Landon's parents caught up with Mr. Carmichael, Landon quietly looked around the event for the Brookdale crew. With the help of a staffer, Landon followed his directions through the house and meandered toward the patio.

Zee immediately spotted Landon, in his worn-in polo shirt and slip-on sneakers, as soon as he entered the backyard. "Landon!" she cried out loudly, catching his attention. He gave a small wave.

Zee walked up to him. "You made it!" she said eagerly. "Welcome to our Christmas in Malibu!"

"Holiday indeed," Landon said. "This is awesome. I feel like I'm in Santa's workshop."

"Cool, right? My mom and I put the whole thing together."

"Nice. Here's a little holiday treat," he said, handing her the gift bag. "Nothing special."

"Ooh, thank you! Anything you bring is special." She peeked

inside the bag and took out a box of chocolates. "Yummy!" Zee said. "Come join us in the gazebo. We're just catching up."

Kathi was the first to spot Landon and Zee walking together toward the gazebo. "Hi, Landon!" Kathi greeted, and reached out her hand toward him. "There's room here to sit down. Join us." Moving mindlessly, Landon inched away from Zee and toward her.

Of course Kathi is trying to move in on Landon. Why is this not surprising? Zee thought to herself. *All she does is pounce on anything I want!* Kathi perked up as she turned to Landon. Zee spoke up then. "I can get you something to eat. You want meatballs? Pasta salad?"

Landon looked at Kathi, then he looked back at Zee. "I am a little hungry," he said. He got up from the seat next to Kathi and followed Zee toward the buffet table near the kitchen.

Zee stole a look back at Kathi and smirked. Kathi smirked right back at her. *It's on now, Kathi!* Zee thought to herself as she walked with Landon shoulder to shoulder to get snacks.

• • •

After grabbing snacks and a frozen hot chocolate with Zee, Landon struck up conversation with Marcus then followed him back to the gazebo, where Kathi was waiting for him. Growing frustrated with Kathi's smothering of Landon, Zee pouted as she hovered by the snack bar, watching them together in the gazebo.

Gabriella walked toward the snacks area, waving to Zee. Zee politely nodded, taking in Gabriella's festive red dress and holiday makeup with just the right amount of glitter. *I'm sure she's never had an awkward encounter with a boy*, Zee thought to herself. *Look at her.*

"Hey, Zee," Gabriella said, looking at Zee's customized Veja sneakers she wore with her red top and white jeans. "Love your shoes."

"Oh, thanks," Zee said, smiling nervously while keeping an eye on Landon.

"Great party! I love the decorations! Your mom said you helped with a lot of it."

"Yep, I did," Zee said, looking quickly at Gabriella and back again toward the gazebo.

"Well, everyone is having a blast," Gabriella said.

"Oh, thanks! You think?"

"Yeah, look at the twins playing on their sled run."

"Right, right," Zee said distractedly.

"So," Gabriella said, following Zee's gaze toward Landon, "is there someone important over there?"

"Oh, um," Zee said nervously. "The blonde guy over there, talking to Chatty Kathi by the gazebo."

"Chatty Kathi?" Gabriella asked.

"Yeah, she's just... throwing herself at him. Landon, I mean."

"Landon is the important one?"

"Yeah, I guess. Anyway, it's so... gross."

"Mm, I see," Gabriella said, looking back at Zee and taking in her face as she watched Landon. Gabriella raised an eyebrow, a knowing smile on her face.

"I mean, do guys really like that stuff?" Zee said.

"What stuff?"

"Like this phony, flirty stuff," Zee said, pointing toward

the gazebo. "Or whatever she's doing."

Gabriella let out a soft chuckle. "Well, I'm pretty sure he knows who is really here for him and who's not."

"You think?"

"Guys can tell sincerity. They may be attracted to one thing, but deep down they can tell when a girl's got real substance or not. And Zee, you have more than enough substance."

Zee looked up at Gabriella. They'd known each other just a few hours. *How could Gabriella know how much substance I have?* Zee thought. "You're just saying that," she said.

"International music star? Superstar party host and clearly still one of the most popular girls at school? Who wouldn't want to spend more time with you?"

Zee blushed, appreciating Gabriella's kind words. *Maybe she's right,* Zee thought. *I do have some good qualities. And Landon did like me before I moved to London. Maybe he still likes me. At least we're friends now. Right?*

"Well," Zee said to Gabriella, "I still have to compete with Chatty Kathi."

"No, you don't," Gabriella said. "To him, it's not a competition. Just watch."

• • •

"Can we have everyone gather near the den, please?" Zee announced to the group eating and drinking on the patio. "We've got a special surprise for you."

Zee and her pals gathered around the grand piano in the room while the parents took seats around the large living area. Mr. P had brought an acoustic guitar with him and passed it now to Landon. "All right, gang, shall we entertain the crowd with a few Christmas carols?" Mr. P asked.

The Beans—Zee, Chloe, Landon, Marcus, and Kathi—started a set list that included "Deck the Halls" and "Santa Claus is Coming to Town." Kathi was on lead, of course, because she insisted. Landon strummed along on the guitar while Mr. P played on the grand piano, and then the crew got together for a rendition of "Lean on Me" that got the parents to sing too. Zee grabbed the mic for the chorus when all the parents clapped along. Chloe put her arm around Marcus Montgomery while they sang, not noticing that he was staring at Zee.

"Niiice... Nice... Everyone! Really great!" Mr. P said when they finished. "What should we sing next?"

Zee could feel everyone's excitement as she looked around the room. She thought about the song she wrote since she arrived in Malibu. She looked at her mother, proudly filming every moment. She took in her friends, her old pals from

Brookdale who she'd spent most of her childhood with, still gathered together like old times, laughing and singing like no time had gone by. Zee felt inspired.

"I've got a little something, Mr. P!" Zee said excitedly. She held her hand out to Landon, who passed the guitar to her. "I've been working on my own song since I arrived, sort of about my holidays over the years. I've never played it for anyone before. But I thought you all might want to hear it."

The gang took a seat around Zee and let her have the spotlight next to Mr. P. Mrs. Carmichael had her phone poised in her hand, ready to record. Zee began strumming the guitar and sang.

"Snow is falling, fire's burning bright.
Mom's baking, it's Christmas movie night.
Candy canes, fairy lights, candles and cheer
Home sweet home
Holidays are here.

This season looks different from the days of old
Everything sparkles like glitter and gold
But the magic doesn't feel the same
Sad to say, it's starting to feel kinda lame.

I don't need fancy gifts, big toys or trains,
Just wanna be near the fire again with you...
With you... with you.
I just want to cuddle close,
Spend time and unwind near the fire again
With you... with you..."

"Woohoo!" the crowd cheered as Zee finished her last note. Mrs. Carmichael wiped a tear from her eye as she recorded the crowd's reaction. Marcus clapped enthusiastically, and Landon gave Zee a broad smile and nodded his head, impressed. Adam and Gabriella cheered loudly and whistled. Gabriella looked over at Landon, then looked back at Zee and winked. Ally and Chloe ran up to give Zee a hug. "Aw, Zee, that was so good!" they swooned.

"All right, gang, one more song?" Mr. P said, dancing his fingers across the piano keys to cue up "All I Want for Christmas Is You." Kathi, Ally, Chloe, and Zee danced in unison in front of the piano, opposite from the boys on the instruments. Marcus tapped a tambourine while Landon took the guitar.

"*And I... don't care about the presents underneath the Christmas tree!*" Zee sang loudly, reaching out to Landon.

Mrs. Carmichael, as well as the rest of the parents, filmed the entire thing on their cell phones, tapping their toes and jamming as the kids sang.

"*All I want for Christmas is yoouuu... Bay-bayee!*" Zee sang, looking at her girls and throwing her arms around them as they closed out the song. The girls laughed and giggled as the parents applauded. Zee stole a glance at Landon and noticed he was looking back at her, smiling.

• • •

As the crowd dispersed to various parts of the house still eating, drinking, and being merry, Zee spotted Landon at the snack bar, caught up in conversation with Kathi once again.

Zee's face drooped, disappointed that every time she wanted to talk to Landon, Kathi always seemed to be there.

Chloe saddled up to Zee. "Girl, don't worry about her. Landon thinks she's so annoying," Chloe said. "She's trying too hard. You know, he asked me about you the other day."

"Really?" Zee asked, her eyes widening. "What did he say?"

"He wanted to know if there was any chance you'd ever come back from London. I was like, I don't know, I guess it depends on her dad's job."

Zee looked at Chloe. She thought about what coming home meant. Was home California? Or Notting Hill? Zee hadn't had that long to explore Notting Hill, but when she returned there on weekends or breaks from school, her bedroom felt more comfortable each time. And here, in California, she wasn't even in Brookdale. She was outside of Brookdale, in Malibu at a rental house, living out of her suitcase. She was on vacation in her own country. She didn't even put up her own holiday decorations in her vacation house, and all the decorations were ordered like take-away pizza. All the homey stuff, the important things, were in London.

"Things actually kind of feel like home over there," Zee said. "I'm finally figuring out how to check the right side of the road for cars, and shepherd's pie is one of my favorite foods now. My mom's kind of found her groove—she's got a whole new set of mom friends. And my dad is killing it at work—he just shot an ad for a really fancy car company. The ad's gonna be on television during the World Cup! We just moved all our stuff over there. I doubt we would want to come right back to where we came from."

"I know, girl," Chloe said. "I mean, look, I miss you like

crazy but obviously know you're super happy. It doesn't matter how far away you are, we're always gonna be close."

"Obviously," Zee said, hugging her pal tightly.

With Chloe by her side, Zee looked around the party. Laughter filled the house. The meatballs were almost gone. Phoebe and Connor waddled around the older kids, many who stopped to hand the twins toys or make them laugh on their way to the snowball toss and slides. Mr. P nodded and smiled as he chatted with Zee's parents.

The house was busy, noisy, messy, and full of joy. The extravagant party that Mrs. Carmichael planned was not what Zee had wanted at first. But now, as she looked at how much her friends and their families were enjoying themselves, Zee was thankful her mother went all in on the festivities and still included some of Zee's ideas in the details.

This actually does feel like old times, Zee thought. *Different times, but still good times.*

13

GOODBYE FOR NOW

As the sun fell lower in the sky just after midafternoon, the crowd started to thin. The goody bags were stacked by the entrance for guests to grab on their way out. Mrs. Carmichael stood near the door to wish everyone happy holidays and thank them for coming. She also made sure to get a photo with all the guests so she could post them on her Instagram feed.

There were still more than half the guests at the party when Zee spotted Ally grabbing her holiday goody bag. "Ally! Where are you going?" Zee asked.

"I just got a text from my aunt saying she was on her way," Ally said.

"But I thought you were gonna stay the night," Zee said. "You, me, and Chloe were going to hang out all night and watch holiday movies."

"I wanted to too, but I guess my aunt is picking me up now," Ally said. "We have a bunch of family stuff going on right now. But maybe I can meet up with you guys another day this week."

Zee's frustration was written all over her face. "But our

reunion! This was going to be like our Christmas Eve! We didn't even put on our pajamas and take photos!"

"I know, I'm sad too," Ally said, her mouth frowning. "But maybe I can come another day. You're here for another two weeks, right?"

Zee looked heartbroken as Mrs. Carmichael walked up behind the two of them. "What's wrong, girls? Ally, is that your aunt outside?"

"Yes, Mrs. Carmichael," Ally said, looking out the front window. "I've got to go. Zee, I'll text you. Thanks for everything, Mrs. Carmichael."

"Okay, of course, yeah," Zee said, stammering.

"Let's catch up this week!" Ally said as she hurried through the front door and down the driveway to the street, not looking back once as she got smaller and smaller in Zee's view. Confused, Zee shook her head in disappointment. She turned back toward the party.

"Honey, you okay?" Mrs. Carmichael asked.

"I thought she was going to stay the night with Chloe and me," Zee said.

"Me too," Mrs. Carmichael said. "And I'm surprised her mom didn't come by. Let me find out what happened. Go back to your guests before they leave. Landon is still here."

Zee walked back through the living room toward the patio and spotted Landon there, looking around for someone or something, perhaps Zee, perhaps another star-shaped sugar cookie. He then turned toward the door and walked inside the living room behind his parents.

"Did you have fun?" Zee asked as she approached.

He turned around and grinned when he saw her. "Yeah, great party," Landon replied. "Really liked your Christmas carol. Catchy tune. Good to catch up."

"Yeah, it's good to see you too," Zee said, her eyes dropping slightly. "I guess this might be the last time we'll see each other for a while."

"Yeah," Landon said. "But it doesn't have to be long before the next time."

"No, of course," Zee replied, shifting from one foot to the other. "I'm sure I'll be back in California at some point."

"Or, you know, maybe I can come visit you in London," he said.

Zee looked at him. Her eyes fluttered. "Yes! That would be cool!" she said. Her mind raced. *Would he really fly thousands of miles to London to see me? That would be amazing!*

Then an image of her friends Archie and Jasper flashed across her mind. She wondered what would happen if either one of them knew about her thing with Landon. *I can barely handle the boundaries and responsibilities of both of their friendships. What in the world would happen if Landon jumped in the picture?* Zee thought to herself. *Would Landon's visit really be cool?*

"Maybe," she said awkwardly. Zee tried to sound enthusiastic. "Anyway, yeah, London is so much fun and I'm sure you'd have a blast."

"Right," Landon said slowly. "Well, hope you enjoy the chocolates."

"Oh yes, thank you. Super kind of you. Happy holidays!"

Landon turned and followed his parents out of the main entrance, toting his gift bag behind him. Zee widened her eyes and shut them tightly, hoping she didn't make things with Landon even more awkward than they already were.

Kathi arrived at the front door right after Landon, as if she were following him out. "Great party, Zee! These goody bags are a nice touch. How classy," she said.

"Thanks, Kathi," Zee said through clenched teeth.

"We're going to be spending Christmas in Aspen, so this is probably the last that I'll see you before you go back to London."

"Great, Kathi," Zee said, unclenching her teeth and smiling. *That's one less awkward encounter I have to worry about for the rest of break,* Zee thought. "Good to see you. Thanks for coming."

"Wouldn't have missed it. Happy holidays, everyone!" Kathi said, waving her hand like a beauty pageant queen as she walked through the door.

Zee rolled her eyes as she shut the door. "Happy freaking holidays, Kathi Barney," she muttered under her breath.

Mr. P and his partner were among the last guests to leave.

They thanked the Carmichaels for their hospitality as they each grabbed a gift bag. "Don't be a stranger, Zee," Mr. P said. "And why did I have to hear about you performing a solo on YouTube? I'm your first mentor! Let's have some regular Zoom calls or something and we can talk music."

"That would be cool! I just didn't think you'd have the time," Zee said.

"I always have time for you," Mr. P said. "Maybe we can even talk about some virtual music lessons if your parents allow."

Zee smiled as she waved goodbye, feeling reassured to have guidance from her old music teacher at the ready even when she was in London.

Chloe ran up behind Zee. "I cannot wait to put on our pajamas and make s'mores in front of the fire! Where's Ally?"

"She had to leave."

"What?!" Chloe exclaimed. "This was our night!"

"I know, I thought so too!"

Zee looked as if she might cry, but Chloe perked her back up. "Listen, doesn't matter. We're going to have the best night ever, and if we have to do a video call with Ally, then fine. Where are your pajamas?" Chloe said.

"In my room."

"Great, let's get changed. We have a whole night to plan."

• • •

Zee and Chloe rang Ally on video conference. "Allyyy..."

Ally answered from her bedroom, looking a bit sad. "Hey, girls."

"Ally, what are you doing?" Zee asked.

"Oh, just sitting in my bedroom again, like I do every night."

"Where is your mom?" Zee asked. "I thought you guys had family plans!"

"My mom has plans, but I don't have plans."

"Okay, then you're joining us. Put on your pajamas! We're taking photos!"

Ally laughed. "Are you serious?"

"Yes! Put on your pajamas right now, we're taking photos!"

Ally disappeared off camera for a few moments while Chloe and Zee waited on Zee's bed. They put on some Christmas music on Zee's phone in the background and danced around.

"Okay I'm ready!" Ally said, wearing the same red-and-white-striped pajamas that the other girls had on.

"Okay, stand still, Ally!" Chloe said. The girls put Zee's computer on the middle of their bed, and Zee stood on one side. Chloe set up her phone on the dresser across from the bed, setting a timer to take a photo of all three of the girls together. "Okay, smile!" Chloe said, rushing to the other side of the screen.

They posed as if they were all together, modeling their matching PJs, giggling and singing along the way. The camera flashed and took the photo. The girls cheered. "This will have to do until our next reunion," Zee said, smiling at the photo.

14

THE AFTER-PARTY

The post-party glow still burned bright the next morning. Mrs. Carmichael left most of the Christmas decorations from the party in place around the house, and the fake snow globes were still floating in the pool. The big sled run had melted down to a suitable bunny hill for the twins, so now Phoebe and Connor each had a sled run their size to enjoy.

Zee and Chloe shuffled out of Zee's room looking for breakfast. "Should we make pancakes?" Zee asked.

"Yes!" Chloe said. "Maybe we can do Christmas tree pancakes. Where are your cookie cutters?"

Zee started to look for the baking tools when Camilla and Mrs. Carmichael came into the kitchen. "Morning, girls," Mrs. Carmichael said. "How are we feeling after the party?"

"Mrs. C, it's all over social media," Chloe said. "Everyone at Brookdale is posting and reposting about it!"

"Great! That means the party was a success," Mrs. Carmichael responded proudly.

"I thought it was a success because we were able to recycle

everything or donate the leftovers to homeless shelters," Zee said. "And my friends were happy. And we got good photos!"

"Well, that too, Zee," her mother said. "Actually, I thought it was great because I saw a smile on your face the entire time. Now, what shall we do about pancakes? Camilla, don't we have those red and green sprinkles left over from the party? Those will be great for a festive touch."

The girls ate their breakfast in front of the television while watching a Hallmark holiday special and reviewing footage of all of yesterday's fun on their cell phones. They uploaded their favorite video clips and photos to the Zee Files in case Ally hadn't seen them.

"I just can't believe how pretty Mr. P's girlfriend is. Did she do something while I was gone?" Zee asked.

"Got a stylist," Chloe said. "She used to dress in only oversized jeans and T-shirts every day, but after a conversation with me, I hooked her up proper."

"You styled Mr. P's girlfriend?" Zee raised one eyebrow.

"Well, not every day, but I did show her a few Instagram accounts I liked that she could take a few pointers from," Chloe said proudly. "After that, she started buying some new clothes and got a haircut, and boom! She's hot like fire. I'm just saying I might have had something to do with that."

Zee laughed. "Let's see what Ally's doing." She pulled up Ally's number in her phone and dialed. "Hey girl, what's up? You awake?" Zee greeted.

Ally appeared on the screen with sunglasses on and blue water behind her. "Nothing. Just chilling by my aunt's pool."

"Where's your mom?"

"Oh, she had to run out," Ally said.

"Huh," Zee said. "Is she ever around? I'm still surprised she didn't come to the barbecue. My mom was really excited to see her and was surprised she didn't even come to say hello."

Ally rolled her eyes and shifted in her pool chair. "Mom was pretty much gone all day and night. And didn't come back until this morning, and then ran out once again."

"Have you guys been spending any time together?" Chloe asked.

"We spent a few days together in the beginning, but then she said she's been busy with work."

"Busy with work during the holidays? That's gotta be really tough," Zee said. "But if she's so busy with work, then why doesn't she just let you chill over here? Your dad was busy and that's why he let you go have fun in California while he worked!"

"Yeah, I know," Ally said. "Anyway, how was the rest of the party? What else happened with Marcus Montgomery?"

"Wait," Chloe said, perking up. "Did anybody hear him talk about me? 'Cause I know he was totally feeling me!"

Ally and Zee looked at each other through their screens. "I didn't hear anything. At any time. To anyone," Ally said.

"Neither did I," Zee said. "And I talked to a lot of people. I was the co-host, after all."

"Hmm," Chloe said. "I guess I'll have to ask around."

"What are you doing today?" Zee asked Ally. "We're going to bake more cookies and hang out by the pool, and maybe ride bikes around. Do you want to join us?"

"I don't know when my mom is going to come back, and my aunt wanted to take me shopping," Ally said.

Zee's face fell in disappointment. Chloe tried to stay

positive. "Well, if you end up going to the mall or something, maybe we can meet you there."

"Yeah, I'll keep you posted. I'll talk to you guys later."

• • •

After a full day of making TikTok videos, riding bikes, hanging by the pool, and baking another batch of cookies for Chloe to take home to her family, Chloe's parents picked her up later that evening, just before sundown. After she left, Zee helped her mother wrap a few gifts for the twins, then hid them at the top of a closet on the opposite end of the bedrooms ("where their little chubby fingers can't find them," Mrs. Carmichael said).

Zee and her parents gathered on the couch to watch whatever holiday special was on TV. Afterwards, Zee went to her room and snuggled into bed. Her mind wandered to all the people she'd seen and the things she'd done on vacation so

far. Brookdale Academy. Chloe. Landon. The party. Zee took out her journal and started writing her thoughts down.

The party—after Mom took my recommendations—was a success. Mom toned down some of the ridiculousness and we had an amazing eco-chic reunion! And everyone came! Ally and Chloe (whoop whoop!), Kathi (meh), Marcus and Conrad (yeah!), Mr. P (awesome!). And Landon came too! We didn't have much time to chat, but we sang together and he said he wanted to come see me in London! Now, if I can find a way to see him without running into Archie, it would be no sweat.

Zee tossed the journal back on the bed. She sighed, thinking about her friends. She thought about how easy and light her conversations with Marcus and Chloe, and even Kathi, were, but how there was still this distance between her and Ally.

Ally hasn't been around as much as I thought she'd be. She and I used to be so close, but lately she's felt so distant. We only got to spend a few hours hanging out together at the party before her aunt had to pick her up. Ally seems like she's trapped at her aunt's house! Why can't she just spend the night with me? I really thought we were going to relive our past holidays. We haven't even gone to Bucks together for peppermint hot chocolates!

I have been gone from Brookdale for months and it was just like old times with most of my friends from my old school. But Ally seemed distracted. I feel like things between us haven't been the same ever since I moved to London, and I don't know why. Maybe between living in Paris and her parents' divorce, she's going through so much drama she doesn't have time for me.

Zee looked out the window. She thought about how when she and Ally were younger, they would spend hours at each other's house, reading, playing with dolls, singing and writing songs, pretending they were playing concerts at huge stadiums like their favorite singers, and talking about what they would do once they made their first album and sold a million copies. She thought about the Christmas they had before Ally moved to Paris. Zee, Chloe, and Ally had spent the entire winter break together hopping from one girl's house to another's, staying up and talking for hours, practicing braiding each other's hair, and watching every holiday movie they could. Now, Ally could only spare a few hours with Zee, and she always seemed preoccupied even when they were together.

Zee looked down at her journal. She took a deep breath, and continued writing.

Is she over being friends with me? Has Ally... outgrown me?

15

ALLY'S SECRET

*T*he day before Christmas Eve, Zee was making a list and checking it twice. Not of things she wanted from Santa (though she'd already forwarded her wish list to her mother weeks ago), but rather of the things she wanted to see and do before she went back to London: *Hot chocolate at Bucks. Watch that Hallmark movie about the three puppies who get separated on Christmas Eve. Make my own glitter. See Chloe again.*

At the top of the list was a sleepover with Ally. Zee begged Ally every day since the party if her aunt could just drop her off one day on her way out. Ally blew Zee off every time.

Finally, Zee made a desperate move—she asked her mother to beg Ally's mother for Ally to spend the night. Mrs. Carmichael called Mrs. Stern and told her how eager Zee was to have her friend over. The two moms had a longer conversation than expected, and Mrs. Carmichael ended up speaking to Ally's mom in private for most of it.

Zee was worried that Ally wouldn't be able to leave the house again. Was Ally in trouble? Was Mrs. Stern really that swamped with work that she couldn't drive Ally to Malibu? After the call was over, Mrs. Carmichael found Zee and told her the news. "Get ready. Ally's coming tonight for a sleepover."

• • •

Zee ran down to the main entry room looking for her friend when she heard the front door open. "There you are!" Zee said. Ally turned around and hugged Zee.

"How do you not get lost in here?" Ally asked, looking around the house as if she wasn't just there a few days ago.

"This isn't Buckingham Palace, Ally. I can see the backyard from the front door. You hungry or something? Where's your mom?" Zee asked.

"My aunt dropped me off again," Ally said. "Mom's out, of course."

"Your mom is out more than my brother who's in college."

"Yeah," Ally said, looking down at the floor.

"Right," Zee said, trying to find the words that would disarm her friend. "Should we go to the patio? Get some snacks, chill in the gazebo?"

"Sure," Ally said.

The two went to the kitchen to grab popcorn and a few juices, then headed out to the patio. They walked toward the gazebo with arms full of munchies.

"Finally, we get to hang!" Zee said.

"Yeah, it's been hard to coordinate schedules," Ally said.

"And your mom seems to be... not around."

"Yeah," Ally said. "It's been kind of, like... bad."

Zee looked at her friend. Ally had seemed preoccupied

since she walked in through the door, and now she seemed downright nervous. Like she had a secret to share.

"I didn't want to say anything earlier, but my mom..." Ally took a breath. "I found out that she has a new boyfriend."

Zee shook her head. "Whaaaa?" Zee said. "Hold on, a *what* now? A *boyfriend*?!"

"His name is Vincent. They met in Paris, but he also has family in L.A. Mom told me about him when I arrived. Like, as soon as I got off the plane. He came over from Paris a few days before us."

Zee tried to process this new information. *Ally's mom has a boyfriend? Like, she's kissing and holding hands with someone who is not Ally's dad? Whoa.*

Ally looked down at her hands. "So when you called me saying you were coming back to L.A. and I should come at the same time you were, my mom was elated. It meant she got to hang out with Vincent in L.A., not just me. As soon as I got here, I realized that she was going to spend all her time with him."

Zee looked at her with wide eyes as Ally continued talking. "Vincent's been over every single day. He always eats at our house and then takes my mom out. Mom and I haven't had any time alone. And I feel really... like he's stepping in as my new dad. It's, like, weird."

"Does your dad know?" Zee asked.

"I have no idea," Ally replied.

"That must be so... strange, right?"

"I don't know," Ally admitted. "I already feel weird. I'm not sure how much weirder things can get."

Zee looked at her friend. Ally seemed to be torn between

wanting her mother to be happy and feeling left out by her mom's new relationship, and also feeling guilty that she knew this information when her father might not.

"What's Vincent like?" Zee asked.

"He's nice. Very French. He's a lawyer. They go shopping a lot. And my mother always comes back home with bags of something."

"Do they bring you anything?"

"Sometimes," Ally said. "But that's not the point. I just feel like my mom has abandoned me. We haven't done anything together. She was barely there on the first night of Hanukkah."

"Ally, I'm sorry," Zee said. She wondered what she could do to make her friend feel better. Zee couldn't imagine her life without her mom and dad together. She certainly couldn't imagine them holding hands and kissing other people.

Just then, Mrs. Carmichael walked into the patio area. "Girls, do you want to go to Bucks for some peppermint hot chocolates? I know they're your favorite. I have to go that way to run an errand, so I can take you."

Zee perked up. Ally smiled, the first time she has smiled with her teeth showing all afternoon. "Yaass, Mom! Let's go!" Zee said.

The girls grabbed their shoes and purses and headed for the strip mall in Brookdale where the local coffee shop was. Bucks has been their meeting spot since they were in preschool, when Ally and Zee went with their moms after school. Mrs. Carmichael and Mrs. Stern would order hot chocolates and later no-caf lattes for the girls, and Zee and Ally would sip them and review schoolwork or play games while the moms caught up on life.

Mrs. Carmichael opened the door to Bucks and Ally and Zee walked inside. "I've been craving a mocha from here myself," Mrs. Carmichael said.

Zee and Ally picked a corner table for them to sit and enjoy their beverages while they watched the hustle and bustle of people walking by doing their last-minute holiday shopping. A few moms wearing black leggings and holding yoga mats waited nearby for their drinks. An older couple held hands as they gingerly walked through the front door.

"See, I thought my parents would end up like them," Ally said, her eyes on the older couple. "I guess not."

Zee's heart sank. "Don't worry," she told her friend. "They still could be."

The girls and Mrs. Carmichael decided to finish their drinks while walking around the mall, passing stores including a jewelry shop and the crafts show. Ally perked up as they walked past the front door to one of the stores. "Oh my gosh, remember those friendship bracelets we made for each other a few years ago?" Ally asked.

"I still have mine," Zee said. "In my jewelry box in London." They peered in and giggled over the fun memories in the store and the designs they would make with the string and beads they saw.

Back at Zee's house, Ally and Zee hung out by the pool until the sun went down and Mrs. Carmichael summoned them inside for dinner. With Ally and Zee, Zee's parents, the twins, Camilla, and Adam, they made for a full table.

Ally looked around. "This is the most people I've had dinner with all week," she said. "This is awesome."

"Just make sure to get a dinner roll before my dad and

brother eat them all," Zee said.

As everyone ate and talked loudly, Zee looked at her friend beside her. "You know, I didn't know what was going on with your family earlier. I thought you were being distant from me because you didn't want to be friends anymore," Zee admitted.

Ally looked surprised. "Why would you think that?"

"I dunno," Zee said. "You're going through so much. And you live in Paris now, which is super cool and chic, and you're doing cool and chic things."

"No," Ally said. "I'm watching other people do cool and chic things from my apartment patio. Because my parents are working like mad and caught up in their own drama."

Zee looked down at her dinner plate. "I just... I'm sorry, Ally."

"It's fine," Ally said. "Yes, it feels like my family is falling apart, and that's tough. But our friendship is what makes me happy. It's the one thing I know I can rely on these days." She gave Zee a small smile before turning back to the lively table. The twins giggled as they smeared food on their plates, while Adam kept their parents entertained with stories from campus life at Stanford.

After dinner, the girls got into their matching holiday pajamas and took more pictures together. They uploaded a bunch to the Zee Files and sent a few to Chloe, who was at her aunt's place for a family dinner. *Darn it, now I'm not there for the photo!* Chloe texted.

The girls camped out in Zee's room, watching a movie on her laptop, then another movie, then raiding the kitchen for Christmas cookies, then falling asleep. In the morning, Zee handed her gift to Ally: the journal, just like hers, that

Ally could use for her essays or other personal thoughts. "It's helped me a ton," Zee said. "You might want to keep ideas for your stories in here."

"Thanks, Zee, that's so nice," Ally said. Then she reached into her overnight bag and pulled out something. "And I have this for you."

Zee was surprised Ally got her a gift. Taking the small wrapped box slowly from Ally, Zee noticed her friend smiling widely as Zee carefully took off the paper. She was hesitant to reveal the inside.

"Open it, Zee," Ally said.

Zee opened the box and pulled out a small frame. Inside was the photo that Chloe and Zee had taken of themselves in their matching pajamas, with Ally on the computer screen between them. Though it had seemed awkward at the time they took the picture, the image nestled in the frame captured an excited, truly happy moment between three friends with

a bond that knows no boundaries—even if they all lived thousands of miles away from each other.

"A memento of our holiday together," Ally said. "Hopefully we'll have more time together next year when things settle down on my family's end."

Zee gave her pal a big hug. "This is so great, Ally! I'm keeping this on my nightstand wherever I go."

Ally smiled. "See, no matter where you are, there I am."

16

TRADITIONS NEVER FADE

Though the sleek, all-white modern Malibu rental looked nothing like Zee's old house in Brookdale or her new one in Notting Hill, the holiday vibe still felt familiar. Christmas Eve and Christmas Day included routines Zee cherished from holidays past.

On Christmas Eve, her family continued their usual tradition of ordering Chinese food. Gabriella came over with Adam, and while they waited for dinner to arrive, Mrs. Carmichael arranged the annual holiday photo with the entire family—including Gabriella—in matching green plaid pajamas.

After dinner, Mrs. Carmichael and Camilla helped the twins leave cookies and a letter for Santa before they got bathed and ready for bed, while Adam drove Gabriella back to her parents' house. Zee took photos with her phone as she watched Phoebe and Connor leave their cookies and letters underneath the tree. The image of the two was so adorable that Zee uploaded it to the Zee Files to share with Chloe and Ally.

Christmas morning was bright and cheery. Zee woke up later than the twins but before Adam to the smell of eggs and coffee permeating throughout the house. She walked toward the hallway, the sound of "Have a Holly Jolly Christmas" getting louder as she approached the living room area. She found neatly wrapped and perfectly styled presents placed under the Christmas tree.

"Santa was here!" Mrs. Carmichael said as she entered the room.

"I see," Zee said. "Did he bring me anything?"

"Zee, you think he'd forget you?"

"I don't know, we've got all these new faces now," Zee said. "The twins, Adam's girlfriend..."

"Zee, no matter who's here, you'll never be forgotten." Her mother handed her a small box carefully wrapped with a ribbon. "This has your name on it."

Zee opened the small box, and inside was a small gold Z on a beautiful gold necklace. As Zee stared at it, Mrs. Carmichael wrapped her arm around her daughter and said, "It's just something to remind you of how powerful you are. Such a bold person that you go by just one letter."

"Aw, Mom, thank you. It's beautiful," Zee said. "I'm going to wear it every day."

When everyone woke up, the family gathered around the tree and passed out presents and toys. Zee helped the twins unwrap boxes revealing their new robots and dolls, and Adam helped Mrs. Carmichael take photos and assemble the new tripod Mr. Carmichael got her as a gift.

Later, Zee heard from Chloe. "Girl! I love the bath bombs! Thank you," she said of Zee's gift to her. Zee had stuck them

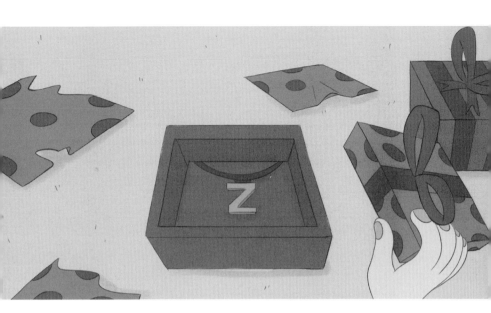

in Chloe's overnight bag during their after-party sleepover. "I also got a new hair crimper and a tie-dye set. We're gonna be busy the rest of break," Chloe said.

"Spa day!" Zee said. "And thank you for the face masks! You know I love them!"

"Of course!" Chloe said.

Zee also texted Ally to see how her holidays were going. *Vincent's here. Again,* Ally replied.

Then out of curiosity, Zee texted Landon. *Just to be polite,* she thought to herself.

Zee

Hi.

A few minutes passed. *Well, it is the holidays,* Zee thought. A few more minutes passed, and still there was no response. *He's probably busy. I bet I won't hear from him. I shouldn't have bothered him anyway. Ugh, now I look desperate!*

Zee placed her phone in one of the dresser drawers, then buried it underneath several pairs of underwear so she could place it out of sight and out of mind.

• • •

Adam picked up Gabriella to join the Carmichaels for dinner that evening. Zee beelined to her as soon as they walked in the house.

"Hi, Gabriella! Come in!" Zee said, grabbing her arm. "Can we talk in private?"

"Sure, Zee," Gabriella said, following Zee to the den near the piano. "What's up?"

"Um, I think I did something foolish," Zee said nervously. "I texted Landon on Christmas night. And now he hasn't gotten back to me. What if he thinks I'm desperate? What if he's not thinking of me at all?"

"Oh, Zee, how nice of you," Gabriella said. "If I were him, I'd probably be tied up with family stuff but feel super glad you texted. And I'd text back when I didn't have any family around me, which can be hard on Christmas night. Give it a few hours, he'll get back to you."

"A few hours?" Zee sighed. "What do I do until then?"

"Chill out," Gabriella said, putting a gentle hand on Zee's shoulder. "Enjoy Christmas dinner with your family. Like Landon's probably doing right now."

Zee looked at Gabriella. "Yeah, I guess you're right."

"Besides," Gabriella said. "I want to hear more about London. Sit next to me at dinner and tell me about life in the U.K."

• • •

The family gathered around the long dining room table for Christmas dinner, which included a honey baked ham, roasted vegetables, and homemade buns. Phoebe and Connor sat in small high chairs between Mrs. Carmichael and Camilla, drawing their attention while Adam, Gabriella, Mr. Carmichael, and Zee passed around plates.

"Mom, you made the stuffing?" Zee asked, referring to the walnut and cranberry stuffing in a large white casserole dish.

"It's your favorite, sweetie. Of course I made it."

Zee smiled. "You really outdid yourself this year, Mom."

"Thank you," Mrs. Carmichael said. "It's fun to cook for large groups, especially when the large group is my kids."

Mr. Carmichael smiled. "Yeah, cooking for just me is really not fun, huh?" he said, winking. He turned to his son. "So, Adam, what happens when you go back to school? You're really doing this law thing, right?"

"Yes, Dad, it's a real thing. And yes, you really will have a lawyer in the family," Adam said.

"Best. Christmas gift. Ever," his father joked. "Just kidding."

California Christmas here looked just like Zee remembered it. Then her mind wandered to London. She wondered what Christmas dinner at her friends' houses there looked like. What was Jameela doing right now? Or Tom? Was Archie having dinner in some castle in the English countryside with a dozen staffers? How about Jasper? Was everyone having the best time ever with their family? Did they all eat together? Was there pie?

Zee leaned back from the table and rubbed her belly. "I

can't believe I'm saying this, but I'm actually quite full."

"Then will you have room for dessert? Your favorite chocolate cheesecake is in the fridge," Mrs. Carmichael said.

Zee's eyes widened. "Wow, Mom, you really did go all in!"

After dessert, the rest of the family helped clear the table while Zee snuck off to her room. She stood in front of the dresser. Though she didn't want to look at her phone, her hand felt propelled to the drawer as if by a magnet. She reached in and looked at the home screen.

Landon had responded back.

Landon

> Merry merry. In Palm Springs. Wish you were here. Hope you liked the chocolates.

Zee smiled as she looked at the phone. Landon's text was short, sweet, and friendly enough. She put the phone back in the drawer, happy she made contact with Landon and content with the brief exchange for tonight.

Zee then grew curious about what her friends from The Hollows were up to. She hadn't heard from her pals in London because she had been so busy in Malibu catching up with old friends here. While she put on a honey and oatmeal face mask, the same kind in Chloe's gift pack, Zee clicked open Instagram on her phone.

Jasper's feed was full of song notes and mixing sessions in his studio (which was his bedroom). Jameela posted pics of herself at her dance studio in London going through drills and routines. On Christmas Eve, she also posted a photo of her family at a beautifully decorated table for dinner, looking perfectly poised in formal clothes. *Jameela's family never struck me as the ugly sweater kind of family*, Zee thought. Then she looked at Tom's feed and found a few mantras and poems about world peace and harmony. *Typical Tom*, Zee thought, *always thinking about the good of mankind.* Archie didn't have an Instagram feed.

Zee went on YouTube next to see what videos Izzy created for her channel lately. Zee knew Izzy had posted vlogs about her holidays at home almost every day since school let out, but Zee had been so busy she hadn't seen many of them. She peeled off her face mask, grabbed a glass of water, then clicked on the first video.

The lively footage included Izzy hanging out with her friends, making cookies, watching holiday movies, and shopping—the same things that Zee was doing in Malibu, except Zee was doing it by the beach.

Zee clicked on one of the most recent videos. It showed Izzy and her family having a holiday party on Christmas Eve. Her family was at the dinner table snacking on holiday treats while Izzy explained to the camera who everyone was and what was going on. The camera turned to the other side of the room where there were some friends and a cousin or two. Then the camera panned across a boy with dark hair. "Wait," Zee said out loud. She rewound the clip a few seconds and looked closely. It was Jasper.

Izzy greeted Jasper, who was wearing a festive red-and-white-sweatshirt, with a kiss on the cheek and a wide smile. Jasper was just as eager to see her. The two looked like they were the perfect little Christmas couple. Jasper had brought her a small box of something, maybe chocolates or cookies, and she took them as she gave him another hug.

What. In. The. World? Zee thought. *Are they... together?*

Zee continued to watch the video. Jasper seemed so comfortable at Izzy's house, greeting her parents and friends as if they'd already met. He took a seat at the dinner table and laughed at jokes and drank some apple cider. It looked as if he and Izzy had spent most of their holidays together, or intended on spending the rest of their holidays together.

They're totally together, Zee thought. *Wow.*

Zee stopped the video and leaned back on her bed. Of all the people in London, she missed Jasper the most. He was the person she was most excited to have more time to hang out with after her breakup with Archie. But from that video on Izzy's YouTube channel, it seemed Jasper was already preoccupied.

So, are they a thing? Like a real thing? She thought about texting him to ask. But it was Christmas night and almost four in the morning in London. She slowly put down her phone.

Zee looked at her guitar, feeling defeated. She had been excited to write new songs with Jasper when she returned to school. She envisioned going to their favorite studio in the music hall, bringing the guitar with her and jamming while Jasper nodded his head approvingly, creating backing melodies along the way. They'd chat and laugh and come up with crazy-good songs that someone would then leak to YouTube, and then they'd get a million hits and a major record label would call and ask them to sign a record deal. *We could have been a regular Shawn Mendes and Camila Cabello,* Zee thought.

But not anymore.

"Like, wow," Zee said to herself. "How things have changed."

17

PACKING UP

The Carmichaels had just a few more days left in Malibu before the family headed back to London. After watching Izzy's Youtube video with Jasper all over it, Zee had been dreading the return flight. *I think I just lost my best guy friend to the most popular girl in year nine,* she thought to herself.

Zee's heart felt a tug. She was just starting to get sort of cozy in California again, having reconnected with friends and enjoyed her favorite treats. Plus, the weather and the beach rekindled good memories. Her mind thought about going back to The Hollows and wearing down coats and boots, and being the third wheel with Jasper and Izzy. Zee shook her head. *All that sounds downright unfun.*

Zee's phone vibrated. It was a text from Ally.

Ally

> I'm off to Paris. I spent a day and a half alone with my mother.

Zee was shocked. She didn't think Ally would be leaving so soon.

Zee

Dang, really?

Ally

Yeah. Vincent was here the entire time. He was at every meal. He was at our house every day. It's not even her house, it's my aunt's house! And he has a house in California! But there he was. In front of me. Every day. Before I had a chance to brush my teeth!

Zee

Oof. So what happens now? Is he going home with you all?

Ally

No, he's coming in a few days. He has to finish some business here first.

Zee

That means your two dads will be in the same place at the same time.

Ally

Don't call him my dad. I have one dad. Vincent's just... a friend. For now. Ugh, this is so weird.

Does your dad know about him yet?

Ally

No idea, but he's about to find out.

Zee

I'm so sad we didn't get to see more of each other.

Ally

I know. Don't worry, we'll see each other in Europe. Maybe I can come to London for spring break. If Mom's gonna spend all her time with Vincent, I'll need to escape from their company somehow.

Zee

Done! Let's plan a spring fling!

• • •

The entire Carmichael crew sat down at the dining room table packed with meats, cheeses, roasted vegetables, and homemade biscuits and puddings. Gabriella sat next to Adam and across from Zee.

"Did he text you back?" Gabriella asked Zee.

"Oh," Zee said. "I almost forgot. Yeah, he did."

"Told you," Gabriella said. "So what now?"

Zee shrugged. "I dunno. See if he buys a plane ticket to London?"

The girls laughed and tucked into the dishes in front of them. Reaching for a biscuit, Zee smiled as she thought about the possibility of having a reunion with Landon in London.

"This looks like the last supper!" Mrs. Carmichael exclaimed when she saw the spread for dinner assembled by Camilla.

"It is the last supper, Mrs. Carmichael," Camilla said in response. "So enjoy!"

"This is our last dinner all together in Malibu, guys," Mr. Carmichael said.

"Well, not, like, *ever*," Zee said.

"Of course not, we'll be back," Mrs. Carmichael said. "Maybe we should make this a regular tradition."

Zee pulled her seat closer to the roasted corn and reached her arm over for an ear as Adam and Gabriella talked about next semester's classes. The twins dug their spoons into the sweet potato mash Camilla portioned out for them, and Mr. Carmichael took a bite of roasted duck and greens as he nodded his head to his wife. Zee felt relaxed as she gazed out at the patio beyond the kitchen, the ocean waves lapping against the shore in the distance.

"I'm going to miss this view," Zee said.

"I'm sure we all will," Mr. Carmichael said. "But looking out on the rolling greens and old trees of the Cotswolds will be nice too."

Zee looked over at him. "Not the same, Dad."

He wiped his mouth. "After dinner, we'll have one last round of s'mores around the firepit before we go to bed, okay?"

"Yes!" Zee said. She smiled at her family gathered around

the table, her heart swelling in her chest as she ate her last family dinner in Malibu.

• • •

Zee turned over in bed, looking out the window at the sky turning brighter with each passing minute from under the covers. She still had some packing left to do, but she was saving it for the very last minute. The rest of the house was awake already, as if eager to pack and head back to their respective homes.

Adam packed up with Gabriella's help and enjoyed one last breakfast together with the family before getting ready to drive to Stanford. Standing by the car, Gabriella gave Zee a hug.

"Thanks for all the great advice," Zee said. "It's good to talk to someone who, like, knows this stuff."

"Of course," Gabriella said. "You have my number, right? Call me any time you want to chat! Don't be a stranger."

"I will, and I won't," Zee said.

Zee turned to her brother. He threw his arm around her shoulder and pulled her in toward his chest. "Miss you, kid. I'll be stalking you on social. So don't do anything bad," he said.

"Adam!"

"I'm just kidding," Adam said. "Maybe we'll come to London for spring break. Mom, that a good idea?"

"That would be perfect, sweetie! Let's look at flights for the spring," Mrs. Carmichael said.

Zee smiled. Between Ally and Adam, and maybe Landon too, it looked like Zee would have a full house for Easter.

● ● ●

Lying on her bed, Zee pulled out her phone and opened Instagram. Her mother's stories were freshly updated. Zee clicked to see the latest video that included highlights from the entire vacation. It opened with a long shot of the food, panning over the yummy dishes they ate during their holidays. Then Mrs. Carmichael got close-ups of the twins, Zee and Adam, and finally Mr. Carmichael and Camilla. There was footage from Christmas Eve and of their matching pajamas photo shoot, and from Christmas, with the twins opening their gifts in the morning and being wowed by what Santa had delivered, and Christmas dinner with the entire family.

There were lots of photos and video clips of the family smiling at the table, laughing at jokes, the twins drooling then smearing food against their high chair tables and laughing hysterically. There was also a shot of Mr. Carmichael giving a cheers, followed by some lighthearted music. *Wait, that song sounds familiar*, Zee thought.

"I don't need fancy gifts, big toys or trains,
Just wanna be near the fire again with you..."

"That's my song!" Zee said. "Aw, Mom!"

The video ended with a shot of Zee and her father sitting around the firepit roasting marshmallows from Christmas night. Then the twins walked in frame wearing their pajamas and looking ready for bed, Camilla following closely behind. Then Adam and Gabriella walked in, Gabriella wearing a red jumper and leggings, looking like a supermodel on holiday, and Adam wearing cozy sweats and slippers. Finally, Mrs. Carmichael walked in and sat next to Zee's father, resting her head on top of his shoulder. The entire family gathered around the fire, roasting marshmallows.

How in the world did she get that shot? Zee wondered.

The video closed out with text in handwritten script: *My biggest and most treasured gifts. All perfect. All mine. Happy holidays.*

Zee dabbed a tear away that formed in the corner of her eye. Her mother successfully curated an amazing and perfect-looking holiday break. Though she did try to art direct every single photo on her feed, Zee knew what made it truly special, and it had nothing to do with fancy photos. Being together was what made it all magical.

18

BACK IN THE U.K.

*L*ondon was just as Zee had left it—cold, busy, full of people bustling around. Remnants of the holidays lingered, with bright lights and decorations hanging in some storefronts and wreaths on lampposts. Still, it was time for Zee to consider her next semester at The Hollows. She needed to prepare for reentry.

She flopped down in the blue bean bag in her bedroom, taking a load off after many hours of travel and dragging her heavy suitcase from the airport back home in Notting Hill. Zee looked at her guitar. "You and I have some catching up to do," she said out loud.

Zee pulled out her journal and read through some of the memories she'd written down over the past few weeks. She already missed Chloe and Ally. And Mr. P. And Landon. "Landon," Zee said out loud. "Wonder if he really will visit me here?"

Then Zee thought about what she was going back to at The Hollows. She wondered what the next semester of classes would be like. Harder? Better? She wondered if Izzy and Jasper were going to come out as an official couple on the first day of classes. Zee felt again a slight twinge in her chest when she thought about Izzy's YouTube video with Jasper in it.

Her eyes drifted to the guitar again. Zee picked up the instrument and started to play. She quickly became lost in stringing melodies and getting in the groove of having her hands on the instrument again.

Suddenly, her phone rang. It rang again and again. It was too annoying to ignore. She fished through her purse and picked it up, focusing her eyes on the caller ID. Archie. Then he sent a text.

Archie

> Cali, Cali, Cali. Are you back in London?

Zee didn't know what to say. She had barely heard from him on break, and now, two days before school started, he was interested to know if she was home. Her heart fluttered. Archie still had some effect on her.

Zee

> Hi there. Where are you?

Archie

> London. Wicked break. Skiing in Gstaad, Christmas in Geneva. Back home for New Year's. Parents bought too much stuff over the holidays and now they're flipping out over where to put everything. Well, really, Mum is flipping out.

> **That's funny.**

Archie

> Yeah. So do I have to wait until school begins to see you? You're in London and I'm in London. We could hang out now. Right?

Zee thought about it. Her heart did that flip-flop thing it did whenever Archie called. Or texted. Or looked at her. She thought about their happy times at Moe's Coffee Shop and jamming away in the music studio. It would be just her and Archie, two friends, hanging out. *I mean, that's what friends do during holiday break, right?*

Zee

> **Well, yeah, but I'm in Notting Hill. How are we going to meet?**

Archie

> I'll have my driver take me wherever you want to meet. Your house?

Zee thought hard. Should she meet him here at her house? *That seems too close for comfort,* she thought to herself. *I don't want Mom and Dad to grill him around the dinner table.*

Zee

> **No, that's OK! Maybe we could meet somewhere close? There's a great place by me with killer sandwiches.**

Archie

> Why don't you meet me at Soho House? Have your dad bring you or I can send my driver to you to meet me there.

Zee thought about it. *That sounds rather posh for a casual catch-up.*

Zee

> Let me ask my parents.

Archie

> We could get a late lunch and then hang out. My treat.

Zee

> Right.

Zee was already exhausted just thinking about the logistics of meeting up. Did she really want to jump into a face-to-face with Archie after a long transcontinental flight? School started in just a few days.

Zee

> Maybe we can just meet at Moe's when we get back to campus. Like old times.

Archie

> Old times? Or good times?

Zee smiled.

Zee

Both.

Archie didn't respond for a few seconds. Then his reply came.

Archie

See you at our usual table, Cali.

Zee put her phone on her desk. She felt reassured that their friendship was back on normal terms.

She looked at her guitar. She picked up the instrument, snuggled into her blue bean bag chair across from the window, and started strumming a few chords. An image of Archie popped back into her head, followed by a flash of them together at their usual table at Moe's.

Zee recited lyrics to herself. *"Some things never change, some ties are unbroken, never frayed..."*

Her heart fluttered in her chest. She shook her head and continued strumming chords on her guitar, smiling.

THE END

Read on to see what happens with Zee and her friends in Book 5 of The Zee Files, *New Beginnings.*

1

NEW ARRIVALS

$\mathcal{M}$ackenzie "Zee" Carmichael's phone was buzzing. The incoming message was short and unexpected.

Archie

I'm outside.

It sent Zee into a tizzy.

She was in her room unpacking the flip flops, shorts, and a few bathing suits still balled up in her suitcase from winter break. The Carmichaels had recently returned from vacation in California, the first time they'd been back to their home state since moving to London in the fall. Zee felt refreshed after three weeks in Malibu living next to the ocean and seeing the palm trees and beaches again. She still had a touch of a California tan on her skin after hanging out under sunny skies.

While in Malibu, Zee had hung out with her best friends Ally Stern and Chloe Lawrence-Johnson, and visited her old school, Brookdale Academy, where she reunited with her old band, The Beans. The Carmichaels even hosted a holiday party at their rental house, which Zee's friends and family described many times over as "epic."

Now, Zee was back in London, reminiscing about the good times she had on holiday. In just a few days, she would be back at The Hollows Creative Arts Academy, back in her uniform with the wool blazer, and the warm California air would be just a memory she'd have while walking to class in the chilly air of the English countryside.

Campus life wasn't all bad, however. In the few months at the boarding school, Zee had made new friends, like her roommate Jameela Chopra and their dormmate, Izzy Matthews, who had her own YouTube channel about life at boarding school. Zee had reconnected with Jasper Chapman, who she knew before as a transfer student at Brookdale Academy before he returned to London to The Hollows. Aside from finding friends, Zee had performed in the school's Creative Arts Festival and went to the fall school dance with her pals. She had also had her first romantic relationship, with Archie Saint John, but that ended almost as quickly as it began. By the time they had left for winter break, Archie and Zee had decided to be just friends.

A lot had happened in the first semester of her new school. *What's next from here?* Zee had wondered.

Apparently, it was a surprise visit, because right now her ex said he was here. In front of her house. Waiting to see her.

Zee had told Archie she'd see him on campus in a few days. *What in mylanta did he mean that he was outside?!* she thought frantically.

Um hi? You're here? How do you know where I live? How did you get here?

I told you I have a driver. And your address was in the school directory. Come outside.

Zee froze. She was not prepared to see an ex-boyfriend. Not only was she still wearing an old sleepshirt and leggings, she didn't want to introduce him to her parents, much less let them know he was outside. She looked around her room, quickly springing into action. She had to do something. She certainly couldn't face Archie looking like she just rolled out of bed.

Zee grabbed a cashmere sweater from her closet, pulled it over her head, then smoothed her long, curly hair up toward the crown of her head and wrapped it into a smooth bun. She put on some lip gloss, took a deep breath, and tiptoed downstairs.

Mr. Carmichael wasn't home, though Mrs. Carmichael was in the kitchen with Zee's twin siblings Phoebe and Connor, along with the twins' nanny, Camilla. Luckily, all were too busy to notice Zee grab her coat and sneak out the door. As she walked toward the front gate, Zee saw Archie standing there on the sidewalk in front of a black SUV with a small wrapped box in his hands.

He smiled at her. "Merry Christmas."

"You're a few weeks late," Zee quipped.

"Better late than never," he said, handing her the box. "Just something small."

Zee took the box and opened it. Inside was a selection of chocolates. She smiled and thought back to her party in Malibu, where her old Brookdale classmate and former crush Landon Beck had also gifted her chocolates. *I guess this is what guys do to charm girls*, Zee thought. *It works.* "Thank you," she said.

"How was your holiday?" Archie asked. "And open the chocolates and try one. They're Swiss."

"California was great," Zee said. "Saw old friends, ate a ton, had a party."

"And you didn't invite me?"

"Didn't think you'd show," Zee said. She took a bite of one of the chocolates. "These *are* good."

"Ah, Cali, I'd have made it," Archie said, leaning against the car. "Okay, maybe not. That's quite a long flight. My driver, Chazz, would only take me across town without telling my parents."

Zee looked up at him, surprised. "Your parents don't know you're here?"

"They're too busy to notice. Besides, I just came to say hello, see how you are, give you this little gift, and, you know..." Archie looked down at his shoes and shifted from foot to foot. "I missed you."

Zee bit her lower lip. Archie knew how to make her blush ever since they first met. While he was known to be aloof and withdrawn to most people, with Zee he was warm and attentive and eager to chat.

"It's nice of you to come here," Zee said.

"You've been on my mind," Archie said. "I've been working on some new music. Maybe that's why."

"Oh!" Zee said excitedly, putting her hand on Archie's forearm without thinking. "I got my guitar back from California! And I've been writing too. Maybe when we get back on campus, we can get those jam sessions going again in the music hall, like we used to."

"Right," Archie said. "I finally get to see you really play. That would be cool."

Zee pulled her hand back to her side and smiled at him. Archie smiled back at her. Then the two looked away from each other. A gentle breeze fluttered through the air and a light snow flurry began to fall from the sky.

The car window lowered and the driver inside said to Archie, "We'd better get back."

"Right," Archie said. He turned to Zee. "I'll see you on campus. Tea at Moe's?"

"Of course," Zee said.

Archie leaned in toward Zee and gave her a quick kiss on the cheek. Then he turned around and got inside the car, while Zee slowly walked back toward her house. She gave a little wave to Archie as the car drove off, then held her hand to her cheek where he had kissed her. Though it was cold enough to start snowing outside, her face still felt warm where Archie's lips met her cheek.

• • •

After a good night's rest, Zee woke up to a quiet Saturday morning. She had no plans on her agenda and therefore no reason to get out of the candy cane–striped holiday pajamas that she had bought to match with Ally and Chloe. *After this weekend, I'll have to put these pajamas away until next year,* Zee reasoned to herself. *So I gotta get every last minute out of them.*

Zee went downstairs looking for breakfast and found her mom bustling around the kitchen, handing the twins toys, bowls, and sippy cups. It was Camilla's day off, so Zee guessed she was still upstairs in her room. Mr. Carmichael was in the den, reading through the papers, watching television, and checking e-mails. Zee joined him on the other side of the couch with a bowl of cereal and her cell phone. A quiet hum settled in the den as the family settled into their morning routine with the local news playing on the television in the background.

Just then, Camilla walked into the den in an excited state, holding a copy of *Hello!* magazine in her hands. "Oh. My. God. ZEE!" Camilla said.

Zee almost dropped her bowl of cereal at Camilla's urgent tone. Camilla rarely raised her voice at the twins, much less at anything.

Camilla then revealed the big news of the day. "Princess Valentina of Costa de Alba is coming to The Hollows!" she said, waving the magazine.

Zee had no idea what she was talking about. "Princess Who of What?" Zee asked, totally confused.

Camilla turned the magazine around to show Zee the article. The page included a photograph of a beautiful dark-haired girl about Zee's age, posing with a man and a woman who looked like royalty. Zee read aloud the headline splashed across the page. "Princess to Posh U.K. Boarding School." She looked up at Camilla. "The Hollows is posh? I mean, we're a school of dancers and poets."

"Zee! Princess Valentina is a big deal, "Camilla explained. "She is the most popular princess in Spain. She's the only daughter of the royal family, and she's going to be at your school, in your same year!"

Zee continued reading. "Princess Valentina of the Spanish island of Costa de Alba is transferring to The Hollows Creative Arts Academy in the Cotswolds next semester to study music. The Spanish princess had formerly attended the Latin School in Costa de Alba but wanted to pursue education outside of her country. Valentina is the next in line for the throne in Costa de Alba. Though she is just thirteen, she's already being groomed to take the helm and lead the country one day." Zee looked back up at Camilla blankly.

"You've never heard of her?" Camilla asked in surprise.

"No!" Zee said.

Zee picked up her phone to do her own research. She pulled up Instagram and searched for Valentina's account, which appeared instantly. Zee found that the princess had a very official-looking profile with her photos appearing more like headshots for a resume rather than casual social photos. Then Zee Googled "Princess Valentina," and found a barrage of news clippings. *I guess she is a big deal*, Zee thought to herself.

The more news articles she read, the wider Zee's eyes grew. She'd never known real royalty before, much less slept on the same grounds as a princess. What if Valentina ended up in the same dorm as her? *Would I have to ask permission to walk by her room every day?* Zee thought. *What if the princess wanted to use the restroom at the same time as I did? Would I always have to leave her alone and suffer through morning breath, or wait for a shower until she was done?*

She wondered what other things would appear on campus with a real princess at school. Limousines and armored cars? Paparazzi? The Queen? Zee had no idea how to even address this new Valentina girl. Princess Valentina? Your Highness? Would she have to curtsy in front of her?

This can't be happening, Zee thought, shaking her head. *There's no way a princess would come to school at The Hollows. Why would she want to go all the way into the English countryside, especially when she could go to school near the ocean?* "Is this really true?" Zee asked skeptically. "Dad, you've said before that you can't believe everything you read. What do you think?"

"Believe it, Zee," Camilla said. "You're going to go to school with royalty."

Just then, a reporter on the local TV news interrupted their conversation: "Royal watchers will be all abuzz as another member of royalty comes to the U.K. Princess Valentina has enrolled in The Hollows Creative Arts Academy in the Costwolds. The Hollows is a small, private boarding school and caters to students pursuing various disciplines in the arts. Rumor has it Princess Valentina wants to study violin and pursue her music study seriously there."

A photo of Princess Valentina appeared on the screen, the same girl who was in the photo in *Hello!* magazine. Camilla squealed with excitement. Mr. Carmichael took off his reading glasses to watch the TV report, then shrugged his shoulders. Zee's eyes blinked repeatedly, trying to take in the news.

Apparently, it was true. A real-life princess was coming to The Hollows.

Acknowledgments

First, thank you to Tina Wells for your continued trust in me to collaborate with you on *The Zee Files*. Creating these books with you has been a dream come true. I treasure our friendship and working partnership.

Thank you to the wonderful team at Target, Christina Hennington, Ann Maranzano, and Kate Udvari, for your unrelenting support and dedication.

Thank you to the West Margin Press team, Jennifer Newens, Rachel Metzger, Olivia Ngai, and Angie Zbornik, for all of your hard work.

To Marc Lavaia, thank you for always looking out for me.

To my family and friends, especially my little lady Quorra, thank you. I love you with all of my heart.

Finally, to the readers, thank you all for your support. I so enjoying hearing how Zee has touched your hearts.

—Stephanie Smith